KISS ME GOODNIGHT

MICHELE ZURLO

OMNIFIC PUBLISHING
LOS ANGELES

Omnific Publishing
1901 Avenue of the Stars, 2nd floor
Los Angeles, CA 90067
www.omnificpublishing.com

First Omnific eBook edition, March 2014
First Omnific trade paperback edition, March 2014

The characters and events in this book are fictitious.
Any similarity to real persons, living or dead,
is coincidental and not intended by the author.

Library of Congress Cataloguing-in-Publication Data

Zurlo, Michele.
    Kiss Me Goodnight / Michele Zurlo – 1st ed.
    ISBN: 978-1-623420-99-4
    1. Contemporary Romance — Fiction. 2. Detroit — Fiction.
    3. OCD — Fiction. 4. Childhood Trauma — Fiction. I. Title

10 9 8 7 6 5 4 3 2 1

Cover Design by Micha Stone and Amy Brokaw
Interior Book Design by Coreen Montagna

Printed in the United States of America

Chapter One

My name is Lacey Hallem, and it's been sixty-seven minutes since my last lie. I'm not a pathological liar, though I do derive pleasure from the act. Usually. My lies aren't intentionally mean, and I don't often go for small ones. Case in point: the lie I told sixty-eight minutes ago? Now I'm paying the price. Or reaping the rewards—however you want to look at it.

Why did I lie? I have no idea. Sometimes I open my mouth and the strangest stories pour forth. I was standing in line at Jimmy John's, my stomach doing the tango with my intestines because I hadn't set my alarm, and breakfast had been the casualty. I just wanted to order my sub and wolf it down. The strip mall housing the restaurant was near the Troy, Michigan, office where I work, which is not all that far from Detroit, and it would have taken more time and effort to drive there, so I walked. April finally seemed to be bowing down to the idea of spring, so it was good weather for a walk.

The nice boy behind the counter handed over my sub, and I promptly unwrapped it, taking a huge bite. As I closed my eyes to savor the ecstasy of vegetables, meat, and cheese product, I realized I had left my purse at work.

Instead of owning up to my mistake, I felt around for my missing bag. Not finding it (because it was still in my desk drawer in my office), I looked down in surprise. While I'm not an actress, I am a consummate liar. I'm not proud of that, but finding myself in the zone where my head buzzes with excitement and my better sense is nowhere to be found, I said, "My purse is gone."

The boy, who looked old enough to have had this job for all of a week, blinked at me. "Gone?"

Frantic now, I looked around. When I commit to something, I go all the way. "Gone. Did the strap break?"

Other people in line began to look for my purse.

I kept going, knowing I was seconds from selling this whopper. "My car keys are in there. My house keys. My diaphragm! I need that!"

I neither needed nor had a diaphragm. My love life is as dry as a desert riverbed, and for good reason, but I'll get to that later.

Putting the now-bitten sandwich back on the counter, I retraced my steps toward the door. "I came in, got in line. Did I have it?"

"Maybe you left it in your car?" The man in line behind me wore a hopeful expression. He eyed my sandwich hungrily.

I widened my eyes as huge as they could go. "Then my keys are locked in there too!"

A woman who looked like she'd recently escaped the clutches of a gaggle of children shook her head in commiseration. Frizzled strands of hair hung from her upswept hairdo, and smudged fingerprints in a variety of bright colors stained her skirt and the lower reaches of her shirt. "Go check, dear."

Another woman asked, "Do you have one of those satellite services that unlocks your car?"

I didn't bother to answer. I might have people who work for me, but that doesn't mean I make serious money. The company I work for is poorly run, and they have trouble keeping people who know how to do anything. I should've abandoned ship months ago. But I'm serious when I say I see my commitments through.

I ran out the door and over to a nearby car, hoping to God it didn't belong to anybody inside. Cupping my hands to combat the glare of the noontime sun, I pressed my face to the window. Nothing.

Returning to the restaurant, I met the gaze of the boy behind the counter and shook my head miserably. The best kind of lie is one

I don't have to tell. I let him and everyone else in the restaurant fill in the blanks however they wanted. By this time, he'd informed the manager, who had my sandwich in hand. "Miss, you go ahead and eat this, and we'll call the police."

Shit. The police. I did not want them involved. They have a way of ferreting out the truth. I can stick with a lie as long as nobody challenges me. But I took the sandwich. After all, what else were they going to do with it?

I nodded bravely. "No tow truck, though. I have another set of keys at home." I washed my palm down the front of my face. "I need coffee."

The fingerprint-covered woman turned out to be an elementary-school teacher. She explained this as she produced a stack of gift cards for the coffee place at the other end of the strip mall and handed me one. "It's on me. Here's hoping your day gets better."

I'd scarcely tucked it into my pocket (again, no purse) before the police showed up, and within a matter of minutes, I had filed a report. I refused to say the purse had been stolen, and I didn't provide any kind of description of a culprit. Similarly, nobody in the restaurant had seen anything untoward (because nothing had happened). I wasn't holding my breath for a call saying they'd recovered my belongings.

Afterward, I headed to the coffee shop. I could have used more than caffeine, but I figured I'd used up my daily allotment of vice. Spreading out my sandwich and coffee, I reflected on the fact that leaving my purse in my office had led to the cancellation of my credit cards. The paperwork hassle was not worth a free lunch. Why did I keep doing this to myself?

And that's not the only sort of thing I do. Also on my list of crap that makes my life harder: every serious relationship I've been in has involved a married man. I started young, meeting my first love when I was seventeen. He was eighteen, and he'd been married for three months. It was a mistake, he told me. I was his one true love—you get the picture. In my youthful naiveté, I bought the whole story.

The next two guys weren't as open about their marriages. I found out they were otherwise involved only after falling head over feet for them. I was a married-man magnet. It didn't help that I lied too. Not about being married, but still...What kind of stones could I throw at another liar?

So, I've done the logical, sane thing. I've stopped dating. If I can only find love and magic with a married man, I'll stop looking for it.

In the meantime, I've collected quite an array of battery-powered boy-friends. Because listening to music is my favorite escape, I've named them after lead singers in various bands. My favorites are Jared (Leto, 30 Seconds to Mars), Simon (LeBon—needs no explanation), and Davey (Havok, AFI—that's A Fire Inside, in case you didn't know). I have a severe crush on AFI. I've named toys after every member in the band, but Davey is definitely my all-time favorite. He lights all sorts of fires inside me.

So, it didn't surprise me that as I got my iced latte and sat down in the coffee shop, my eyes were drawn to a particular man who looked to be in his mid-twenties, waiting just outside the door. His outfit straddled the border between punk and goth: battered jeans and a well-washed AFI shirt. (Bonus for him, I swooned at the shirt, never mind that it looked incredible on the man in it.)

A chain linked his wallet to his belt, and it swooped down to the middle of his thigh, drawing my attention to his legs. Mr. Hot-ness wasn't exceptionally tall or anything. I'd say maybe five-eleven, although measurement estimation is not my thing. I work well with hard data, not suppositions, and I'm rather on the vertically chal-lenged side, so up is up, damn it. His black leather boots seemed to add a few inches. I'd recognize vintage Doc Marten's anywhere, though I personally no longer dressed like a kid rebelling against my parents. My mom had been too understanding—even with my lying. There'd been nothing to protest.

The place was packed, not that it took much to fill it up. Like me, others had picked up Jimmy John's from down the way and brought it over to eat while they sipped coffee. The only remaining open seats were near me, and I sat at the corner of a long table, which could seat maybe twelve. Remember, my estimation skills stalled in second grade. It could've held eight, and I wouldn't know differently until I tried to seat the ninth person. The coffee shop might let us bring food from other places inside, but their cramped and limited seating clearly said they didn't want us getting comfortable and staying long.

No matter. I didn't have much time to loiter. I'd already stretched the limits of my twenty-minute lunch break. The owner of my com-pany was in the hospital, lingering after a massive heart attack. His son was in town, and the current rumor had him downsizing the company in order to sell it. I really needed to reassess my loyalty. If I got fired today, I had money put aside, but my résumé wasn't ready to go, and I hadn't even begun to think about looking for another job.

Mr. Hotness held the door open for a tween boy, who ducked under his arm and squeezed between him and the door. The kid was one or two growth spurts away from being the same height, and he forced Mr. Hotness—probably his dad—to dance to the outside. I laughed at the way he shoved him out of the way to enter first. I probably looked like an idiot, sitting alone and chuckling out loud. Of course, I wasn't all that alone. The woman sitting next to me shot a weird look over, obviously worrying about my mental health.

I flicked a smile at her in assurance. I know I'm a little messed up, but isn't everybody? Laughing is certainly not the weirdest thing I could do, and I usually come off as confident and independent, or at least I try to. As you've seen, I've brazened out a few situations in my time and later, from the comfort of my sofa, wondered what the hell had come over me.

"Hey," Mr. Hotness protested, but he didn't sound mad. His voice carried above the din—a scratchy, melodic cadence that would sound sexy in the dark. He could give my Davey a run for his batteries. The glare he directed at the boy held too much amusement to be effective.

The boy shrugged and darted toward the back of the place with a mischievous grin. His smile and the gleam in his eyes matched his father's, and I saw a replica of the tween heartthrob Mr. Hotness must have been.

He got in line. More people came in. The seats across from me opened up, and I stared out the window, watching the traffic whiz past. I'd sworn off married men, especially those with children. That was just another reason to halt my nefarious activities. You might argue that I had no proof he was married, but the fact that I was attracted to him was proof enough. My radar is seriously fucked up. At least it matches the rest of me.

The woman to my right stood, as did her friend, and once they left, I was officially flying solo. There was no one left to camouflage the fact that I was *sans* company.

The thing is, I've never minded eating alone. No need for small talk, and I hate talking to people as they check their phones. Nothing tells me I'm unimportant like watching someone LOL to a text while I'm trying to uphold my end of the conversation. *Hello*, people! In person should count for something.

Within minutes, Mr. Hotness appeared on the other side of my table, blocking my view of the road. I was struck by his teal eyes. I hadn't expected them. The color seemed too bold to be true on the surface, but when I looked more closely, I saw flecks of blue and green. His midnight hair, longish, falling over his forehead and curling at the ends, made their color stand out even more.

He smiled—a friendly one, not a wanna-fuck one. "Are these seats taken?"

I wouldn't have minded seeing the wanna-fuck one, though he was clearly with his son, and blatant flirting, even if he was divorced, would be crass. I didn't see a Mrs. Hotness or a ring anywhere, but men this yummy didn't stay single for long. And again, the fact that I found him attractive spoke volumes. I might be seeing his face tonight in place of Davey's. Sorry, Davey. Oh—maybe Mr. Hotness and Davey together, both of them focused completely on me. That fantasy bore further exploration.

I shook my head. The thought of those lips wrapped around pink parts of me banged around in there, but eventually clattered away. I did not give him an inviting smile, though I was tempted. He oozed sexy badness, and whoever says they don't have a weakness for that has a serious case of the pants-on-fire syndrome.

The boy slipped behind the row of occupied chairs and stopped next to Mr. Hotness. He came up to the middle of his father's chest, and I estimated his age at about twelve. That one threw me for a minute as I did the math. Mr. Hotness looked like he was in his mid-twenties, about my age. The numbers worked out if he'd started out as a teen father. I'd made my share of mistakes, so I didn't judge.

The kid grinned at him. "Hey, old man. Where're we sitting?"

"Here." Mr. Hotness set down two drinks and pulled out a chair. "Go ask Audra for—Oh, never mind. I'll get it myself."

The boy sat down, and his father disappeared. The woman who replaced him was no larger than the boy. She was blond and cute, two things I am not. Even in a baggy shirt and leggings, she and her rosy glow managed to attract more than a few glances.

For a moment I had no idea why I was feeling guilty. I hadn't done anything except plan to imagine his face and those broad shoulders hovering above me in the privacy of my bedroom. *Imagine*, not invite. Fantasizing is not a crime. However, reporting a theft that hadn't happened is a crime, and the more I thought about *that*, the guiltier I felt.

I shifted and focused on my food. If I hadn't been so hungry, I might have taken it and left. The weather was exceptionally nice. But

I know my limitations. I wish I could walk and eat, but multitasking like that is dangerous for someone like me.

So, when he returned, Mr. Hotness took the seat next to me. His scent—spring wind, clean, a little spicy with a hint of soap—hit me first. I wanted to bury my face in his neck and inhale his goodness. His arm brushed mine when he slid his chair closer to the table. He flashed an apologetic grin. I caught it from the corner of my eye, but I didn't acknowledge it. The muscles in his arms were well-defined, strong without being bulky. And his skin was warm. I tingled where he'd touched me.

Damn me. Why can't I just find a nice, single guy for once?

I ate, and they chatted. Apparently, the wife had been playing softball. Dylan—she called him that, so I went with it—and the kid had watched. They dissected the practice session. Every now and again, a part of him would touch me. His elbow or his arm came into contact with my arm twice. His leg bumped mine three times. It happened too often to be coincidental. If this was flirting, it was much too middle-school for me. But mostly I hated the way my heart rate sped up every time it happened. The atmosphere grew warm, and my nerves were starting to show. I felt another lie coming on.

I finished my lunch, gathered my trash, and reached for my purse without looking. My dexterity is iffy in the best of circumstances, and lusting over some woman's husband while sitting so intimately close is definitely not an ideal situation.

Because my purse was still in my desk at work, I didn't find it on the table. Instead, my wayward hand and frayed nerves knocked over the remaining half of my iced latte, and the river headed straight for his lap. My wad of six unused napkins wasn't sufficient to sop up the mess before it waterfalled off the edge of the table.

Horrified, I turned to follow its path to the floor. Six inches to the left and the stream of coffee would have splattered on my feet. I would have greatly preferred that.

"I'm so sorry." I grabbed napkins from the person on the other side of him and went to dab at the mess, but I froze when I saw exactly where it had pooled.

He looked at my hand, a slow, lopsided grin spreading across his lips and glittering from his eyes. He took the napkins, his fingers brushing against mine and generating more tingling. Why did this have to happen to me? I wanted lunch, not a dose of unrequited lust that turned me into a blistering idiot. I started shaking. My breaths came faster as I fought down a panic attack. I had to get out of there.

"I'm sorry," I repeated, squeezing the crumpled paper wrapper from my sub more tightly. I was close to losing it in a public place, something I'd successfully avoided for years. I needed to regroup. My hands itched, and I fought not to tell him I was legally blind.

He didn't stop grinning. "It's okay. No big deal."

"Monty, go get more napkins." The cute blonde leaned across the table and swiped at the place where the remnants of the pool dripped over the edge onto his lap. Yep, she was definitely a mom, well-versed in cleaning up these kinds of spills.

Monty ran for the counter. I fled to the restroom.

Nobody else was in there, and I was grateful. I was about to engage in a whole lot of hand-washing, and I didn't need witnesses.

Six times, I promised myself. Only one set of six. I had crumbs on my hands, if not the wetness of coffee soaking through napkins.

And so I washed. Once. Twice.

A knocking at the door nearly derailed my concentration. "Hey, are you okay in there?"

It was him. He'd followed me to the bathroom. Why not his wife? That would have made far more sense—not that I'd expected anybody to come after me. It wasn't like we were friends.

"Fine," I called. "Just washing my hands."

And then I had to start over. The ritual had to be perfect the first time, or I might as well flush away the rest of the day. I was on the third cycle when he interrupted again.

"Are you sure you're okay?"

If I answered, I was going to have to start over. I ignored him.

"I'm coming in," he said.

The door opened before I could decide whether I needed to freak out while washing my hands. This was my go-to compulsion. I couldn't change my pace, draw it out, make it go faster, or it wouldn't count.

Lying would have assuaged the stress, but after this morning, I was determined to stop. Again. Never quit quitting, right?

"Are you okay?"

I couldn't look up, but I could see him in the periphery of my vision. "I'm sorry. It was an accident."

"I know. I was there."

I heard his amusement. I counted the fourth cycle, breathing the word out loud to make it official. I needed him to stop talking to me. I couldn't do two things at once, not correctly. I needed to concentrate.

"It's okay, you know. I'm not mad. I've had worse things dumped on my lap. At least it wasn't hot."

I nodded, muttering, "I'm sorry," and, "five," the words piling on top of one another and threatening to ruin my ritual. I should offer to pay the cleaning bill, but I knew his clothes were wash and wear. That AFI shirt was vintage, though. It had the *Black Sails in the Sunset* logo and had to be at least fourteen years old.

He watched me for a blessedly silent moment, but then he put his hand on my wrist just as I started on number six. Good God, he ruined everything! I was going to have a meltdown in a public restroom standing next to a strange and utterly sexy man. Most men would've left at this point, even among of those crazy few who would have followed me in here in the first place. Not Dylan.

"Breathe."

He had an authoritative tone I couldn't ignore. I breathed. I finished number six. "I'm fine. I just need to wash my hands."

He shut off the water and snagged several paper towels. "You washed your hands."

And he'd ruined my ritual. I dried my hands and tossed the towels in the trash. "I have to start over."

"You have OCD?"

It wouldn't take a rocket scientist to diagnose my condition, though most people would have chalked it up to quirkiness or lunacy. "Yes. Please leave. I need to start over."

He didn't respond to the desperation in my tone, and he didn't seem fazed by my impending implosion. He kept his tone light and neutral, like a shrink would. "How about you try this instead: Close your eyes. Take a deep breath."

Amazingly, I did what he said. I'd been in counseling — behavior modification therapy — for this. I knew the drill; I was just having trouble accessing the process. Or remembering to use it.

"That's it. Another."

I don't know how much time passed, but the edges of panic receded and my shaking stopped. I opened my eyes to find him regarding me with a patient smile.

"I'm Dylan."

If I'd had my purse, I would have taken the hand cream out and squeezed the perfect amount onto the center of my palm. "I'm Lacey. And I need to get back to work."

My real name is Alice, but I hate it. When I arrived at my second-grade classroom and saw that my teacher had put "Alice" all over everything I was supposed to use, I threw a fit. I made my mother take me home because I am not Alice. I'm not a huge fan of Lacey—I'm not even sure how it's a nickname for Alice—but at least it's an improvement.

I pushed past Dylan, but he caught me, his hand hot on my skin. "Wait."

I didn't mind being touched. That wasn't a trigger. I took a chance and looked into his teal eyes. "You do know this is the ladies' room, right?"

His eyes lit. "*That's* what the figure wearing the skirt on the door meant."

Sarcasm is one of my favorite forms of communication. I couldn't help it; I laughed.

He smiled. "You have a very nice laugh."

"Thanks." Reaching out, I fingered the sleeve of his shirt. It was a flirty move, and against my better judgment, I meant it to be. Part of me wanted to tear off his clothes and throw him to the floor. "AFI is one of my favorite bands. I'm truly sorry about the shirt."

"It'll wash." That smile didn't fade. He watched me touch his shirt.

Before things could get more awkward, I stepped around him and reached for the handle on the door. "Thanks for talking me down. I hope your shirt doesn't stain."

Chapter Two

When I returned to the office, I washed my hands six perfect times. Stress followed the water and white froth of soap down the drain. Nobody bothered me. Nobody ever bothered me at work unless there was a problem with their paycheck, which rarely happened now that I was in charge of the department.

Some people might think I'm nuts, but my propensity for running the numbers six times has actually resulted in the elimination of most of the problems in payroll. In the last year, I've successfully transitioned us to a new system and straightened out the way we're doing health care and retirement deductions. I'm all about the cost effectiveness.

Oh, I could go on about this all day, but I'm sure you, like my colleagues, are bored with the topic by now and barely amused by my enthusiasm. So I'll keep it to myself. Davey, Jared, and Simon understand. They get a charge out of my enthusiasm. Suffice it to say, I could roll around in numbers and have multiple spontaneous orgasms. Just think about the phallic nature of the number 1. I like to write it thick, with a big base. Think of it as a clitoral stimulator.

I checked my appearance in the mirror over the sink. My hair fell just below my shoulders, curling in perfect ringlets. Other than putting some anti-frizz stuff in, I don't take a lot of time with it, so when it turns out good, I'm always pleasantly surprised. I swiped a napkin under my eyes. Stress tends to make my mascara smear, and that just makes me look tired.

I'm not bad looking. Some have even called me pretty, and I don't disagree. My eyes are large, but not too big. I have a cute nose, and the oval shape of my face has a pleasing symmetry.

I straightened my shirt and smoothed my skirt. The cut of both pieces emphasized my curves. I left the restroom feeling positive about myself, and that's always a good sign.

My office assistant, a shaggy, skinny, awkward-looking man in his early forties, waylaid me as soon as I made it back to my department. Alec is a good-hearted person who never quite got over his Dungeons and Dragons phase, and I'm not sure he's all that acquainted with the multiple grooming heads on his shaver. On the weekends, he dresses up in an elaborate costume he made himself and meets up with friends to act out games.

I'm not judging. He has a few good friends. That's really all anybody needs to be happy. And he can sew. I have a few pairs of pants that could use hemming, but I haven't worked up the courage to ask him if he'll do it for me.

"Ms. Hallem, Mr. Pritchett, Jr., dropped by a few minutes ago. He wasn't on your calendar." Alec lifted his thick brows. His hazel eyes blazed with concern.

What I wouldn't give to have him manscaped. I think he could be moderately cute if he tamed his facial hair.

It's true that Mr. Pritchett wasn't on my schedule, but I'd never admit to being concerned. Downsizing meant my job wasn't safe. Nobody's was. "What did he say?"

"He said for you to call him when you got back."

I heaved a sigh, a big one. Before I could think about washing my hands again, I headed into my office and dialed Junior.

My call went straight to voice mail. I left something short and crisp that probably sounded uptight, worried, or bitchy. I worried about the first and last options, wishing I could erase the message and try five more times.

A man I assumed to be Mr. Pritchett, Jr., appeared at my office door about thirty seconds later, as if he'd been lurking, waiting for my call, and then sprinted in my direction as soon as the phone rang. He came in and closed the door. I could see Alec pacing by the long, thin window next to the door, and he shot me an anxious look.

Boss Junior didn't look that old, which surprised me. Given that his father was seventy-two, I expected B.J. would be at least forty-five. I really should stop trying to estimate. *Counting* is my forte. I need to go with it.

Poised to disarm him, I put on a welcoming smile, willing myself to feel it in my bones so it would appear genuine. As I've said before, I'm damned good at this. My ploy must have worked, because surprise flitted across his face. His smile lit his eyes — pale brown like mine — and turned them a little lighter, the yellowish undertones making them glow a bit. He was moderately handsome. His light brown hair was clipped short and carefully styled, as was his goatee. I wanted to show this manscaping to Alec, to hold him up and say, "See, Alec? See what a little extra shaving time gets you?"

B.J. was average height, which meant he towered over me, and he wore a suit. Crisp, clean lines hinted at definition in his shoulders and hips. By all standards, he was attractive. Suave, sophisticated, rich, and probably built, he was totally anybody-with-a-pulse's type. Yet I was neither attracted nor overly impressed, which meant B.J. was single. A quick glance at his left hand showed no evidence of him ever having worn a ring.

"Ms. Hallem, I need to meet with you."

I lifted a superior brow. This was probably the only chance I'd ever have to get away with that kind of display. "Alec can set up an appointment for you."

He laughed at me, but at least he tried to cover it up by coughing into his hand. "Now is good."

He wasn't very boss-like. The rumors swimming around the building had built him up to be some kind of heartless jerk. Maybe he was like an SBD fart: silent but deadly, creeping up on me when I least expected. I hoped I wasn't about to be Dutch-ovened. I shrugged and gestured to a chair in the corner. If he was going to sneak up on me, at least we could sit down before I suffocated.

I really didn't have meetings in my office. It was meant to house one person, and it did that beautifully. I was the head of payroll, a department of three. That didn't lend itself to holding meetings. I attended them, but I did not call them.

B.J. dragged the chair close and set it near my desk. His gaze wandered across my highly organized workstation. If he stopped to count, he'd find six of everything. Or multiples of six. My OCD wasn't *that* bad. Twelve packages of yellow sticky notes, eighteen pens, or my favorite, thirty-six paper clips.

He crossed his ankle over his knee and drummed his fingers on his thigh. When he looked at me, a hint of pink stained his cheeks as he studied my face. "Pritchett Incorporated has more employees than it can afford. Business isn't as good as it was ten years ago."

I was in high school ten years ago. I wasn't sure about B.J. We stared at each other in an odd silence. The air should have crackled with tension. After all, I was pretty sure he was firing me, but the room did not grow heavy with the weight of my impending doom. I think we both found this development odd. If I had to pinpoint anything developing in the air between us, I'd have to go with a different kind of friction. That unsettled feeling in my tummy returned, though it was not as acute as it had been earlier with Dylan. Based on the way B.J. looked at me and then away, I guessed he was experiencing the same malady.

As we studied one another, I became aware of him as a man. I shifted and put some serious energy into resisting the urge to play with my hair or smile coyly. If we'd been in the coffee shop, I think he would've struck up a conversation culminating in a request for my phone number, and I would've given it to him.

B.J. rubbed his thigh, drawing my attention there, and picked at some lint on his sock—again, not very boss-like. "We're downsizing to make the company salable. The alternative is to just close up shop."

His tone was closer to "Hey, I like you. Want to grab coffee?" than "You're about to lose your job." I had no idea how to take that, so I ignored his tone and responded to the meaning behind his words.

"You," I corrected him. "You are downsizing. We are being downsized, fired, terminated, let go, forced to retire." I could have gone on, but from the way he paled, I think I got my point across. A lot of that friction circled the drainpipe.

"Look, I know I'm not the most popular guy around here, but this should've been done years ago." He actually appeared apologetic while maintaining an alpha vibe. I found the dichotomy interesting and a little exciting.

But seriously, I've had enough excitement for today. I need to keep things calm for at least a few hours. And I could do that if B.J.

would step out of my office and make an appointment with Alec for another day.

I rolled my eyes and heaved one of my famous (in my own mind) sighs at him. "Look, B.J., if you're going to fire me, just do it. Whatever justification you need to sleep at night, go ahead and drink it."

His mouth fell open. I don't think anyone had reacted to him this way before. His uncomfortable, fidgety act probably made the others think they had to make him feel good about firing them, although to my knowledge nobody had actually been fired yet. But there had been a lot of talk, and most people who hadn't already left were floating their résumés around and putting vacation plans on hold.

So why haven't I? Great question. I have no answer.

He managed to position his mouth into a frown. "B.J.?"

I lifted a saucy brow. That's right, my body parts are brazen. As a package, I'm not so confident, but in pieces, I'm freaking awesome. "Boss Junior. What were you expecting?"

From the awkward way he blushed, I knew he'd gone where I hadn't, and this confirmed that he'd been admiring me. "I wasn't expecting that. Most people just call me Thomas. Or Mr. Pritchett."

"I thought your name was Jacob, same as your father."

He winced. "I prefer Thomas."

I can relate to that.

Putting both feet on the floor, he leaned forward and clasped his hands together. "Look, Alice, I'm not here to fire you."

"In that case, you can call me Lacey. Nobody calls me Alice. Alice doesn't live here, ya know?"

From the baffled look on his face, clearly he didn't. "Lacey, look—"

"You say that a lot. Is it a nervous affectation?" Like I have room to throw stones. If there were a sink in here, I'd be washing my hands. He might not be here to fire me today, but there's no safety net for tomorrow or next week.

He pressed his lips together. It was good to know an opponent's lines, limits, and tells. It looked like I'd found Thomas's.

"Lacey, my father asked me to get this company into shape for sale because he can't run it anymore, and none of his offspring want it."

"I'm sure that's not true." Oh, here I go. This isn't going to end well. "He probably has scores of illegitimate children out there who would jump at the chance to run this place."

Thomas's eyes widened for a split second, and he opened his mouth as if to say something before closing it and taking a moment. It was a sign of his good breeding that he gathered himself enough to ignore the tone of my remark. "I have two half-sisters. One is a stay-at-home mom, and the other wants to be a fashion designer. None of us wants to run a company that packages and ships things."

"What about me?" I lifted my hands, palms out. "I'll run it. I'd be damn good at it. Dad never acknowledged me before. Maybe now that I want to carry on his legacy, he will." A tear welled in my eye.

Damn it! So close. So freaking close. Why couldn't I finish this day without drama? Why did yet another thing have to test my resolve?

He blinked. The words were not sinking in.

"Oh, screw it." I grabbed my purse and started shoving personal items into it. A few company pens might have been in the mix. "I'm so tired of trying to get his attention. I've saved this company a ton of money. I've been here long enough to prove my worth, to prove I can be the daughter he's always wanted."

More tears leaked from my eyes. I was into it now. I do love dramatic performances, even when I'm the one giving them.

Thomas stood and closed his hand over mine, putting a halt to my hurried packing. It was the second time today a man had thrown me off guard by restraining my movements.

"Lacey, what are you talking about?"

I looked up, right into his eyes. Misery seeped from my every pore. "Your dad knocked up my mom, and I'm the result. He's paid her off for years. She kept it from me, but I found the letters, the contract that made her keep silent or he'd stop paying her. She needed that money! We were poor!"

Now he got it. His entire face transformed with shock. He staggered backward and plunked down onto his chair. "I knew my dad slept around, but I never dreamed I had another sister out there."

Well, that sure took the wind out of my sails. I hadn't expected him to believe me. I'd met his father. He was the grandfatherly type, always friendly and professional. I could more easily see him dressing up as Santa Claus than seducing a platoon of women. I sat down on the edge of my chair. Folding my hands together, I stared at them somberly. "Tell me what's really going on, Thomas. I deserve to know."

He rubbed his hand over his face, suddenly looking exhausted. "I came to get salary reports. We're closing down. Within a month, this building will be for lease."

I picked up my purse and threw a stapler into it. "Well, then I'm not sticking around. I quit."

He watched me leave. I didn't turn around to make sure — that would have ruined my exit — but I felt his gaze boring into the back of my skirt, most likely concentrating on the sway of my ass, as I went. I'd walked out on two men in one day. Both encounters had left me tingling, and neither was likely to result in anything.

Hell of a Monday.

On Friday, I found myself in court. No, not because I lied to Thomas. This hearing had been scheduled a month ago because I'd been caught walking a dog without a leash or license, and I'd chosen to fight the ticket. Alec had called me Tuesday to say the ax started falling after I left. I'd wanted to warn him, but I have a tendency to veer off topic when I'm upset, and by "off topic" I mean I lie. Who knows what kind of whopper I'd have told Alec if I'd tried to warn him?

So I didn't.

I also refused to feel bad. When I left, I'd held my head high and walked out with my dignity intact, letting people draw their own conclusions. Sometimes that's the better lie.

Court moved slowly. Of course, it would have moved much more quickly if I hadn't sat here for three hours before someone told me I had to take a number. Then the judge adjourned for lunch before he got to me.

I found a Starbucks, but no Jimmy John's. With limited options, I ended up getting a sandwich from a local deli. This was a new experience for me. I'd only ever gone to chain restaurants before.

As a point of habit, I went to actually eat at Starbucks. Long and narrow, this one was even smaller than the coffee place near Pritchett Freight Services. I was lucky to find a table with a view out the front.

That's when He of the Teal Eyes appeared. He'd been on my mind a lot this week, when I wasn't preoccupied with how to format my résumé so each section consisted of six lines. Not many men spent time on my mind. Even Thomas's sculpted face had faded from my memory. Dylan, however, sent my heart and libido into overdrive. Thinking about him usually drove me to spend some quality time with Davey, which reminds me—I need to pick up more batteries.

He (Dylan, not Davey—I would have fainted if Davey Havok showed up) sauntered into the shop. There was an open seat at my table. It's worth noting that many other tables also had open seats. People seemed to be eating in odd-numbered groups, but all the table/chair arrangements came in even numbers. This put me in a bit of a sticky spot.

Speaking of sticky spots, my mouth went a little dry just looking at Dylan. Today he wore long shorts with a colorful plaid pattern. It was a horrible design, but somehow he made it look great. The way they hugged his firm ass probably had something to do with this. I also saw that I was right about him having long legs. Long, sexy, strong legs that could hold me up in the shower while we…ahem. Time to stop lusting after the hot married guy who kisses like a god in my fantasies.

His shirt, vintage Nine Inch Nails—and by that I mean *Pretty Hate Machine*, not any of the regurgitated tracks they've been pushing off as new for the past ten-plus years—stretched across his shoulders in a way that emphasized the solid musculature going on there.

He looked around as he came in, automatically searching for precious seating as he took his place in line. There was plenty. Really. But instead of noting that and minding his own damn business, his gaze fell on me and stayed there. I think it took him a few moments to place me, but then a slow grin spread across his face, and all I could think about was how those lips would feel as they worked their way down my—*Alice Hollie Hallem* (I totally didn't luck out with names), *you stop that right now!*

In the cool of the overly air-conditioned coffeehouse, I fanned myself. The barista greeted Dylan, and he turned toward her as I sipped my iced latte. Should have gone for something warm. At least then I'd be able to explain the flush staining my chest.

While I continued trying not to have wet daydreams about a certain married male, my mind wandered to the memory of the way his skin had felt on mine. My stomach did a flippy thing that felt curiously good. At this point, I wasn't sure if the memory was actually that good, or if I'm suffering the effects of my drought. Either way, that's a depressing thought, so I stopped thinking it and distracted myself by counting passing cars instead.

Plus, I really didn't want to see him. When you accidentally spill coffee all over a hot married guy and then display crazy OCD tendencies in the ladies' room, you never want to encounter the person who witnessed your folly ever again, no matter how hot he is. Even if you slipped up two nights ago and moaned his name instead of Davey's. The vibrator didn't stop performing, so clearly it didn't care. The universe has a sick sense of humor.

A figure blocked my view of the traffic, which was probably a good thing because I'd lost count and that frustrated me. Of all the half-occupied tables, Dylan chose mine. Seriously, dude. Leave me to my misery. I wouldn't have minded ogling you from across the room.

He smiled, calm and welcoming, as he slid into the chair across from me and settled his coffee and muffin on the table. "We meet again."

Immediately, I looked at my coffee, assessing how much was left and the likelihood of it landing in his lap should I suffer another unfortunate mishap.

I wanted to mumble another apology, but he stuck out his hand. "Dylan."

Was he senile? I already knew his name. How could I forget? What the hell. I shook his hand. He had a good grip: firm but not too firm. He didn't try to trace his thumb across my wrist or anything like that, but he still managed to light sparks where I wished he wouldn't.

"Lacey." I'm sure my smile was strained. I extracted my hand. It tingled, and I did not have the urge to wash it. "I remember you."

He tore off a bite-sized chunk of his muffin. Blueberry. "I wasn't sure. You left so suddenly. I didn't think I'd ever see you again, but here you are."

Yes, here I am, once again having lunch with a sinfully sexy married man. The universe is conspiring against me. I wish to hell it would stop testing my resolve. I was serious when I swore off married men.

"And here you are." Wonderful reply. I'm so witty sometimes. Maybe now I should spill my coffee on his lap and run out the back door. Another morsel of that muffin disappeared into his mouth. I wanted to lick the crumbs from his fingers.

He smiled like he knew what I was thinking. "What brings you downtown on such a nice day?"

"Court," I said. "I've been caught flouting the leash laws, and now I have to pay for my crime."

He nodded in commiseration. "They take actual money *and* screw you by making you take time off work."

I didn't currently have a job, so that second part wasn't a problem for me, but it very well could be for most people. I was tempted to spin a yarn about the issue, but in a curiously uncharacteristic move, I found myself unable to tell the lie. I coughed, choking on the words.

Dylan thought I was choking on the bite of my sandwich. He waited, an expression of watchful concern on his face.

When I finished my coughing fit, I took a sip of coffee. "Thanks for not pounding me on the back." I hate when people do that.

"It doesn't usually help."

The rest of that muffin disappeared between his luscious lips, and I could only conjure a vision of him working on another muff—mine: his head of gloriously dark hair perched between my legs, his teal eyes looking up to make sure I was enjoying what he was doing. *Ahhh, Davey. I'm going to need you tonight.*

"Do you know where The Majestic is?" he asked.

I pointed to my left. "About three blocks that way. Are you headed there?"

Color rose up his neck and stained his cheeks a very masculine shade of pink. It was cute. He tried to divert my attention by finishing off his coffee. It didn't quite work. "I'm performing there tonight. I'll be meeting my band in about half an hour. If you stop by after you dazzle the judge, you could check out our rehearsal."

If it dresses like a rock star, apparently it is a rock star. I leaned closer, gooseflesh making its way up my spine. "Tell me you're an AFI cover band, and I'll sleep with you."

Chances are, if he kissed me with enough passion to fulfill the promise his eyes kept making, I'd sleep with him anyway. No dating, though. I had to stick to my guns on at least one part of my pledge. That way I could hate myself a little less in the morning. Ahh, check it out! I'm lying inside my head instead of blurting them out. Does that count as progress?

His breath caught. It's a heady thing to see—a man who can't breathe because of the way you're looking at him. He licked his lips, and I tracked the move with my predatory, home-wrecker senses.

"We're not a cover band, but we play a wicked version of 'Endlessly, She Said.'"

I sucked air like an excited idiot. It couldn't have been sexy, and maybe that made up for flirting with someone I should be avoiding. "Do you mean every word?"

He grinned, and my heart did a few illegal flip-flops. "Every one."

I liked that he played along. I could have bantered Davey's lyrics all day, but I suddenly remembered where I was and what I was doing. The urge to wash my hands pressed down upon me, a heavy, familiar weight.

Bad Lacey.

Sometimes routine can calm me down: I had coffee after breakfast and with lunch, which was again a sandwich. It had been tasty, and now every time I ate one, I would be lusting for this piece of heaven. I grabbed for my coffee, my hand darting out, and of course I knocked it over.

Dylan's reflexes were better this time. In one smooth motion, he scooted back and escaped the path of my favorite liquid. He was a quick learner. I threw a stack of napkins on top of it, hoping to catch the leading edge before it hit the floor. Dylan threw another stack on, and together, we avoided catastrophe.

"I'm so sorry. I'm not usually so clumsy."

"Can I get you another cup?" He flashed a smile, one that said he found my propensity for spilling coffee on him amusing instead of annoying. I would be annoyed if someone kept spilling coffee on me, no matter how cute he was.

I shook my head slowly, as if he'd asked another question, one I both wanted him to ask and dreaded hearing. The coffee was Fate's way of telling me to stop tempting her. "I've reached my quota for the day. Any more and I'll turn into a coffee monster."

"Coffee monster?" He pressed his finger to his muffin wrapper, gathering the sugary crumbs.

"Yeah, you know. Jittery, stays up all night, turns into a hag in the morning. I try to avoid showing myself in such an unflattering light." In a perfect world, I would be able to drink six cups a day. Because it wasn't perfect, I made do with two.

He nodded sagely. "I've both met and been that monster. However, I just can't see how light could fail to flatter you."

Damn. He was good. Those teal eyes never strayed from my face, which was a shame because the V of my shirt emphasized the curves of my breasts. I actually looked pretty good today. The weather had even cooperated, keeping the humidity low so my curls didn't kink up and frizz out.

Heat didn't rise to my cheeks at his compliment. I'm not much of a blusher, mostly because I don't care what people think about me. I did grow warm, however, because being near Dylan lit fires inside me that my beloved Davey might need help quenching tonight. I might have to break out Jared. My boys could work in tandem.

Dylan was so sincere—and in a public place too. Maybe I'd been mistaken. Maybe he wasn't married. I decided to dig in a safe place. I started with his son.

"So, you're flying solo today? No kid?"

Shades of confusion washed over his face. He frowned, staring at me. Finally, he shook his head. "I don't have a kid. Why would you…? Oh. Monty isn't mine. He's my nephew."

The look on my face must have communicated my disbelief.

"No, seriously. He sometimes calls me 'Pops' because he thinks it's funny how much he looks like me." Dylan leaned closer, beckoning me to join him in conspiracy. "I'm only fourteen years older than him."

He didn't seem like the kind of guy who would deny having a son. He'd been openly affectionate with the boy. Okay, then. He was married to the hot blonde, and they were childless. After all, he'd called her "Audra," not "your mother."

I drank in his face, up close and personal. He was less than four feet from me, and I could see every fleck that made up the improbable color of his eyes. I memorized the shape of his eyebrows, even noting the slender scar that ran through the right one. His cheekbones were high and angular, giving his face a square-ish shape. The strong line of his jaw helped with that as well. His hair fell over his forehead, and I wanted to brush it back to see what kind of hairline he was hiding.

If there'd been time, I would have counted every piece of stubble on his face. Fortunately for both of us, I came back to myself with a jolt. I jerked up, sitting hard on my chair. I hadn't realized I'd lifted my bottom as I'd leaned forward. Now my ass hurt. Self-flagellation isn't my thing.

Served me right. I folded the wrapper that had held my sandwich and shoved it in my empty paper cup. "I have to get back to court. It was nice to see you."

As I stood, he grabbed my wrist. It wasn't a harsh gesture, but it managed to be forceful. "Will you come by afterward?"

"Maybe. If it doesn't run too late."

He released me, and I wished he hadn't. He had a firm, sure grip, and I missed the feel of a man's hands on me. He settled back in his chair, that flirty smile on his face. "You can come to the show, but I probably won't have a lot of time to spend with you."

If he was rehearsing, he wouldn't really be spending time with me either. Perhaps I'd found a loophole. Damn. I hadn't been hunting for one. I nodded and fled. I'm not good at ending conversations, especially those I'm not sure I should be having.

Had I just made a date with a married man?

Chapter Three

The dog I'd been caught having out without her leash isn't mine. Sadie belongs to my stepfather, John. I have trouble talking about him for a lot of reasons, none of which has anything to do with him. I haven't been the easiest stepdaughter, but he's never lost patience with me.

I think I would die if he did. Of all the adults in my life, he's the only one I can talk to without worrying about what I say. He knows I lie. He knows when I lie and usually why — even when I don't — and he's taught me to be pretty self-aware. John is a singular human being, and I owe the fact that I function as well as I do to him.

Enough of that, though.

In court, I lied instead of pleading guilty, which I should have done because I did take Sadie off her leash and let her roam free right in front of a sign that warned of the penalties for doing so. Had I seen law enforcement in the parking lot watching? Yes and no. I saw him, but I didn't notice him. It's really not the same thing.

I opened my mouth with every intention of pleading guilty. Earlier intentions aside, I had caused enough trouble for the time being. But then I said, "She was dying, your honor. She was dying, and she wanted one last run around the park. She couldn't even run, really. She just shuffled along."

Though she hadn't wandered far that day, Sadie could run circles around me when she chose to.

Tears poured from my eyes. I put my hand over my heart. "She died that night, your honor. We went home, and she looked up at me with her sad eyes. She could hardly see me through her cataracts. Then she licked my hand, laid down on the floor next to her bed, and died."

I broke down, barely whispering that last part. The bailiff caught me and put me in a chair. She clucked soothing sounds until my sobs subsided to hiccups. She must have been a dog person.

The judge stared at me like he'd seen one too many hysterical females. He wasn't old. I pegged him at somewhere around thirty-five, which meant he saw me more as a piece of meat than a daughter. I prefer to play the daughter angle, but if I'd found him at all attractive, I might have flirted. I can flirt and cry. Fake emotion isn't difficult. It's the real stuff that bewilders me.

He paged through a few documents and cleared his throat. "Ms. Hallem, the license of the dog in question does not match your address, and it doesn't have your name on it."

Well, I didn't have a dog. I probably should have just said so, but could I take the easy way out? Nope.

I straightened up. "She lives with my mother. My apartment doesn't let us have dogs. So, the license is in her name, but Sadie was my baby. My mom is quite frail. She has a wheelchair, but she hates to use it, so she doesn't get out often. I took Sadie to the park every day." I swayed a little and slumped back in the chair. The stress of discussing my deceased companion was too much to bear.

Sadie is actually very much John's baby. She's also alive and kicking. She might be old, but she's healthy and tenacious. So is my mother.

With an aggravated sigh, the judge dismissed my case and gave me a stern verbal warning. But when an authority figure buys into my bullshit, it just encourages me. That's one reason I didn't tell John and my mom about the ticket. John would've come with me and done all the talking. He would've known I'd feed the judge a lie, and he was quite good at making me tell the truth. I'm convinced he's the real reason my mom didn't throw me out by the time I was sixteen.

Lying is like washing my hands. Sometimes I just have to do it. I wouldn't call it a compulsion, though, because it actually soothes me. Truly, it does. And anyway, people with compulsions can't help themselves. I can. Or maybe it's the other way around? In any event, I don't take medication for it, so it's not that big of a deal.

After court, I meant to go home, but I found myself walking past the parking garage and in the direction of The Majestic. I'd been to the club before. It wasn't historic, and I didn't see anything majestic about the faux-wood paneling on it that some enterprising person had painted teal. And not a startling shade of teal like Dylan's eyes. The hue had been dulled and weathered by time, and now it hovered somewhere between trendy and dive.

The front door was open, so I went inside. In the brightness of the daylight and with all the interior lights turned on, it looked a lot different than I remembered. The lobby—where brief, friendly body searches happened—needed to be scrubbed down, but it was neat and tidy, and someone had recently vacuumed.

I opened the next door and stepped into the main room. It was a large area with a smallish stage suitable for local acts. It featured a dance floor and several long bars. Small, round tables scattered along the periphery. If The Majestic had other rooms, I wasn't aware of them. But they had to, didn't they? A business needed an office, and a stage meant storage and at least one dressing room somewhere.

Glancing around, I identified the likely doors and fire exits. I'm not the kind of liar who causes problems by shouting "fire" when there isn't one, but I do like to know how to leave a space. And I know I'll need to use the restroom. I haven't washed my hands since before appearing in front of the judge.

The room was deserted, but there was equipment set up on stage. After a minute, I saw someone—not Dylan—cross the stage and bend down to check something on the back of an amp. He exited without seeming to notice me.

Then a man came through the front door. He was older than me, and I pegged him in the mid-fifties range. He was attractive in a weird George Hamilton sort of way, so I figured he was married. He smiled and set his case on the table to my left. Then he extended his hand. "I'm Craig, the rep from Hanover. Before we get down to business, can I use your restroom?"

Placing my hand in his, I gave him a friendly smile. His grip was heavy, so hard it squished my metacarpals together uncomfortably. That kind of handshake didn't communicate confidence and strength.

It only showed that Craig was an asshole. He couldn't be unaware that he was hurting my hand. Did he think I would buy his shtick better if I was afraid of having to shake hands with him again? Or did he think he'd established control of the situation?

I've heard from a variety of sources that we judge a man by the quality of his handshake. If that's so, I detected no quality in this man.

I infused my voice with frost. "Of course. Let me know if we're out of hand soap in there." I pointed a helpful finger in the direction of the restrooms. "It's flu season."

It wasn't flu season, but I figured he was too stupid to know that. I read a lot of articles online, including a study citing the number of people who lie about washing their hands: ninety-one percent say they did it, but less than twenty-five percent actually do. Thinking about that made me want to go wash *my* hands. Who knew where his had been?

He tossed a leather binder on the table and hurried off in the direction I'd indicated. I watched him go for a second, but curiosity was killing me. I had to know what was in the folder.

You might call me nosy, but I prefer curious or inquisitive. They're better synonyms.

The top document was a spreadsheet showing the volume prices of various liquors. The next document showed the same information, only the prices were cheaper. The third spreadsheet showed an even better deal. So Craig was here to sell booze to the bar. I scanned the numbers, automatically committing many of them to memory. The markup on liquor was *that* amazing.

Another man came in the front door. His bald head gleamed under the lights, and I estimated him at about five-eight and two hundred pounds. I bet he ate a lot of the fried foods available on the menus that perched in holders on The Majestic's tables. He saw me and sighed. The reaction was brief, and he hid it quickly behind a professional smile, but I caught it.

"You're from Hanover?" he asked.

The smile on his face fascinated me. I could tell he had experience dealing with people who wanted something from him — admission to his club, a free drink, access to his stage.

I wanted nothing from him, but his impatience was a challenge to me, and the fact that my hand still throbbed from Craig's crushing grip didn't deter me either. I extended my hand and gave him my most brilliant smile. I didn't have to dig deep because the situation gave me honest joy. "Lacey Hallem."

His polite façade slipped for a minute. I like to think my bubbling enthusiasm cracked his veneer. He shook my hand. Where Craig had an overly harsh grip, this man, who probably managed The Majestic, had a loose, limp thing going on. Both were off-putting, but this one didn't hurt.

"Ms. Hallem, I'm a busy man. You have five minutes."

I cupped his hand between mine, compounding my friendly approach, and stepped closer. Not creepy close, flirty close. I'd dressed for court in a skirt and blouse. I looked demure and cute, yet confident and competent. Lying and manipulation are all about appearances. Any spy can tell you that.

What's the difference between a liar and a spy? That's worth pondering. If I ever meet a spy, we can compare notes.

"Sir, I noticed you don't have your liquor displayed correctly."

He narrowed his eyes. It would help if I knew his name. Saying it out loud once or twice — but not too often, as that's creepy — goes a long way toward solidifying a lie.

"And you're an expert in that too?"

I've seen my fair share of *Bar Rescue* episodes. I inclined my head toward the central bar. "Do you mind?"

He motioned toward the opening. "It's your five minutes."

I surveyed the setup and mentally compared it with what I'd seen on television. "First, you need to display your goods. Customers want to be able to see the liquor. You want your most expensive ones on the top tier. It's subliminal. Short men and those with self-esteem issues will gravitate toward them, if only to make the bartender pull them down to their level."

He had shelving, but he had other supplies on it. Bottles of liquor were lined up on the counter. The napkins, stir sticks, and umbrellas should go elsewhere. I rearranged a few things.

"We used to have it like that, but some of the female bartenders complained they couldn't reach it." He came around the counter and surveyed my handiwork. Then he pitched in and helped me move things around.

I let him do the majority of the work; otherwise he would've realized I had no freaking idea what I was doing. "Invest in a few step-stools, sir. They won't complain once they start making more in tips."

"I need to get more business in here. Last year or so hasn't been great for us."

Guitar sounds twanged over the speakers, and I glanced at the stage. Dylan stood near one of the amplifiers, tuning his strings. Guys in bands are hot. No matter what instruments they play, they generally have strong hands. If they're used in the right ways, I'm a huge fan of strong hands.

"I get mostly local bands playing here. Sometimes I get a smaller tour through."

I nodded thoughtfully. "Are they any good?"

He shrugged. "Sometimes."

"Sir—"

He cut me off. "Call me Mike. That 'sir' stuff makes me feel old."

I lowered my eyes and tried to blush. I might not have been successful, but sometimes the right posture is all you need. "Sorry. I meant it respectfully." And I hadn't known his name.

He touched my wrist gently. It wasn't a flirtatious gesture, just one that let me know he liked me. "I know, Ms. Hallem."

Looking up, I gave him another brilliant smile. It's a good one. Both my mom and John agree that it's one of my best—and worst—assets. "Mike, when I hear a crappy band, I leave a bar. I can see that you envision The Majestic as a place that promotes great local bands and excellent drinks. Hanover can help with that. They offer a variety of liquors, and they also can provide staff training on how to upsell the beverages."

Mike scratched his chin and regarded me thoughtfully. Then he went back to rearranging his bar. "I like you, Ms. Hallem," he concluded after a while.

"Lacey, please."

"Lacey, then. I think Hanover finally got it right, sending you over. Talk to me about prices."

Over the next few minutes, Mike and I proceeded to talk about several things other than liquor. I won't put them down here because I didn't want to hear about how his divorce drained his finances and his son couldn't figure out what college to attend, so I'm sure you don't either. Believe me when I say I did my best to come across as sympathetic, and I think I was successful. I also did work cost information into the conversation.

A man cleared his throat behind us. Loudly. He had to in order to be heard over the guitars and drums doing their sound check. Dylan's voice came over the speakers. I couldn't tell if he could sing from the way he said, "Check, check."

A strange man sat at the bar, and Craig stood just behind him, beta-male style. Wrinkles of confusion made lines between his brows, and he also frowned, making premature lines on the rest of his face. Because I hadn't forgiven him for his asshole handshake, I was tempted to comment on his wrinkle-making habits. But I didn't. Mike thought I was a nice girl, and I was playing up that angle.

I am a nice girl, but I know how to be a bitch too.

The man with him studied me. He was older, silver-haired, and suave. His dark blue suit jacket was cut great and emphasized the breadth of his shoulders. I couldn't guess his age, but I can tell you he definitely worked out.

Mr. Silver-Hair rounded the bar, extending his hand to Mike. "Mike MacMurtry, I'm Dawson Hanover, owner of Hanover Distribution."

Mike shook his hand enthusiastically. "Mr. Hanover, you have one hell of a sales rep here. No pressure, yet she gets her point across. It's been a pleasure to do business with her."

I edged away. The owner of the company might know I didn't work for him.

Mr. Hanover slung his arm across my shoulders. He did it in a nice way, but his firm grip let me know I wasn't going to get out of this cleanly. I hoped to hell Dylan hadn't noticed me yet. Maybe I would come back tonight to see his set.

"You're right. She's amazing. I've been listening to her for about ten minutes. I think she's sold some of my liquor to me."

I gave him an affectionate smile. He seemed nice, and I didn't want to blow this for him. Craig didn't rate consideration, but I already liked Mr. Hanover. He reminded me a little of John, only older.

I know you must be thinking I'm nuts to not break down and beg for forgiveness or make a fun for the door, but I wanted to see where this situation would lead. I've never been arrested for lying because I've never done so maliciously. In general, I don't damage anything but friendships.

And even though I've alienated more than my fair share of people, I've managed to retain a core group of close friends: Jane and Luma. They've learned to spot my stress triggers. Also, if you ask me if I'm lying, I'll admit to it. Always. Jane says I'm hard to love but so worth it.

"Well, I'll let you two discuss the particulars," I announced. "Mike, do you mind if I stick around and watch the band for a little while?" The size of my balls is amazing. No fear — not when I have absolutely nothing on the line.

Mr. Hanover released my arm. "That sounds like an excellent idea. You and I can talk afterward."

I drifted off and let the men discuss the financial side of the deal. Some of the prices I'd quoted Mike were from the cheaper and cheapest sheets. I think that helped keep his attention. When he'd told me what he was currently paying, his rates mostly matched those listed on the most expensive spreadsheet.

Dylan didn't notice me until I was about twenty feet from the stage, which just shows how much he was concentrating. The large dance floor was adjacent to the stage, and I had to cross a lot of open space to get to him.

He looked up. His eyes widened a little, and the corners of his mouth curved in a jerky smile. He'd just started singing, and I didn't expect him to stop, which he didn't. I stood in the center of the dance floor and watched his band play a song.

It wasn't one I'd heard before, so I figured it was an original. I closed my eyes to better absorb what I heard, and I didn't love it. Music feeds my soul. At one point, it functioned as my only emotional outlet, and John had encouraged that by taking me to many live shows and talking to me for hours about how music is constructed. Melodies seep into me and fill the vast silence. Well, good music does.

As I listened, I tried to figure out what was off. Dylan's voice was pretty good. Rich and smooth, it washed over me. I liked the rhythms too. So, what was wrong? As I tapped my foot in time to the drum, it came to me. Without thinking, I hoisted myself onto the stage. I traced the black cords of the bass back to the source, and I turned up that amp. Then I turned the lead guitar's down just a notch.

More than one of the four band members glared at me, but they continued playing. Dylan regarded me with an expression that mixed outrage and bafflement. It was a cute look on him. Some people might have used the word *ominous*, but not me. My spider sense is finely tuned, and I rely on it heavily.

I sat on the edge of the stage and slid down. It was too far to jump and not hurt something. When I resumed my position and closed my eyes, the song sounded better. The layered rhythms were well balanced, complementing Dylan's voice instead of undermining it. Now all he needed were some backup singers. His bandmates needed to pitch in, but I didn't think they'd take that advice from the crazy stranger who'd adjusted their settings.

As I absorbed the song, it changed back to the way it was. I opened my eyes to find the bassist and keyboardist throwing twin glares at me. I shrugged. It was no skin off my nose if they wanted to sound like shit. They played two more, and I identified the same problem, which they apparently had no interest in fixing.

When the last song ended, Dylan leaned his guitar against an amp, jumped down from the stage, and crossed to me.

His eyes flashed, and I knew he wasn't happy with what I'd done. My ballsy behavior probably didn't fit with the shy woman he'd met who freaked out about spilling coffee on him.

"Lacey, you can't just come up on stage and mess with our equipment."

I studied him intently, noting the way his jaw flexed and his lips pressed together. From the periphery of my vision, I looked for him to clench his fists. He didn't.

"Okay."

He waited a beat, two beats. I didn't blink or step back. Finally, he shook his head. "Aren't you going to apologize?"

"No. You sounded better after I made the change and worse when you changed it back. The acoustics in this place suck, and you have to account for that in your mix. I don't see a soundboard, which is a mistake if Mike is serious about featuring better talent."

By this time, the others had joined Dylan. Besides the two male guitarists, the drummer turned out to be a taller woman with an athletic build, long dark hair, and a lip ring. She looked enough like Dylan to be his sister.

I faced the hostile crowd without changing my expression. "You also need backup singers."

The drummer snorted. "I told you so."

Dylan flashed her an impatient look. "Daisy, hush." Then he returned his attention to me. "Next time just say something. Don't mess with my equipment."

I've never had a man tell me not to mess with his equipment. I know that wasn't what he meant, but I couldn't stop from giggling.

Dylan had a hard time holding together his stern expression, and Daisy didn't even try. The other guys were checking out my outfit and trying to figure out who I was.

"Lacey, we need to have a chat." Mr. Hanover appeared at my elbow. He eyed Dylan's unfriendly bandmates with a stern expression of warning.

How sweet. Dawson Hanover was my protector. I barely refrained from calling him Dad.

Dylan scowled at Mr. Hanover, then looked back at me. "Lacey?"

I felt bad because now he thought I hadn't come by to see him. Then again, maybe that was a blessing in disguise. I shouldn't have come by to see him.

"Dylan, this is Dawson Hanover. He's a liquor distributor." I gave Mr. Hanover a hopeful smile. "Did you close the deal?"

He dropped the overprotective parent look to give me a grin. "After the way you set it up? Absolutely. You're amazing, Lacey. You've accomplished what six of my best sales reps have failed to do, and you made it look easy."

Lying *was* easy. The truth is hard.

"Oh, good. I'm glad. Dylan invited me here to listen to his rehearsal." I realized my mistake. Now I was sorry. I faced Dylan with a sad heart. "I'm sorry. You're right. You didn't invite me here for feedback." I reached out and squeezed his shoulder as part of my apology. I absolutely was not feeling him up. "Best of luck tonight."

With that, I turned and followed Mr. Hanover across the floor. It looked like Craig had already left. I halted abruptly. "I need to use the restroom."

The fixtures in this bathroom were clean but worn. Mike needed to do some upgrades if he wanted to attract a different clientele. Perhaps he'd pour some of his liquor earnings into the bathroom.

I stared at myself in the mirror above the sink, the fluorescents making me look pasty, though I knew I looked fine in natural light. Another upgrade. Women don't need to see a crappy reflection when they're trying to look good while sweating in a too-warm bar on a crowded dance floor. My eyes—brown, in case I haven't said—had a sparkle of excitement in them that gave me an impish air.

Lying would help me wiggle out of this situation. I hadn't meant to draw so much attention to myself. I turned on the faucet and wet my hands.

The door opened, and Dylan stepped inside. He watched me, not interrupting my ritual right away. He looked at me in the mirror, and I was too focused on what I was doing to care what he saw.

"I didn't mean to upset you."

He hadn't. I was about to be busted for lying. "I'm nervous about talking to Mr. Hanover."

Dylan crossed his arms and nodded. "You don't have to talk to him, Lacey. I can go out there and get rid of him."

I lifted my gaze from the observation of my third cycle and met Dylan's in the mirror. My knight in a vintage NIN shirt. I don't think I've ever had anyone offer to fight my battles. "Thanks, but that's not necessary."

"What does he want?"

I started on number four. "I'm not sure. He can't be that upset, though. I think I made him a lot of money today."

"He's your boss?"

Funny fact: John noticed early on that I tend to lie when presented with an open-ended situation. He asks me lots of yes-no questions. I shook my head. "I just met him."

Dylan frowned. "Don't leave the building. Insist on meeting with him here."

That was sound advice. "Okay."

"How did court go? Did you pay your fine?"

Cycle five. "The judge let me off with a warning." I did not explain my courtroom shenanigans.

"We're playing tonight. Do you think you can come?" He chewed his lip.

I wanted to chew his lip. I thought about that, and about the fact that he was married and his sister was in his band. I shrugged.

"It depends on what my friends want to do. I think we're going to a movie."

We hadn't yet agreed on which one, and that meant we might end up at one of our apartments doing Jell-O shots or making margaritas. Or both.

His gaze flickered away, and he didn't bother to conceal his disappointment. "We go on at midnight, if you want to stop by after."

I finished with cycle six and felt much better. "I'll see what they want to do."

Dylan handed me several paper towels. "Was the mix really that bad?"

"You sound better with less lead and more bass. It complements your voice. Backup singers would also help, especially in the chorus."

I deposited my paper towels in the trash. Dylan tucked a strand of curls behind my ear. I looked up to find him regarding me with a mixture of fascination and wonder.

"I do appreciate your feedback. Nobody outside the band has heard us play yet."

A joke about his stage virginity would have been funny right then, but butterflies stampeded in my stomach. I needed to get away from Dylan. Being close to him was too much temptation for me to bear. "You know we're in the ladies' room again, right?"

He looked around as if this were the first time he'd realized what went on in a women's bathroom. Spots of color crept up his neck. "Sorry. I figured you were washing your hands. I just wanted to make sure you stopped."

I took another step away. "And what would you do if I didn't?"

He tilted his head and studied me. "I don't know. You don't look frantic anymore. Did that guy make you upset or was it me?"

"Mr. Hanover might not be entirely pleased with me, and I'd rather not go into the reasons."

Dylan nodded, accepting my evasion. "Like I said, don't leave the building with him. I'll play around with the sound while you have your meeting. That way you won't truly be alone."

Chapter Four

It turns out Mr. Hanover wanted to offer me a job. I tried to tell him I wasn't qualified to be a sales rep, but he only laughed.

"Lacey, you weaved a great story; that's all a salesperson does. You helped Mr. MacMurtry see how the Hanover Company could improve his business. Some of your facts were wrong. I did correct those for Mike. But considering you've had zero training, that's to be expected."

He set me up to shadow another rep — not Craig, thank goodness — and go through a training program. I start Monday. Helluva week. I had to fill out an application and take my résumé to Human Resources for them to keep on file.

I was sure he'd check my references, so I didn't include any, and I hope Thomas Pritchett doesn't answer the phone when they call my last place of employment. The last thing I need is for a lie that netted me a job to expose one of my poorer, more dramatic, too-desperate lies.

I'm not proud of the one I screamed at Thomas. I know I should apologize, but I don't see where that opportunity will arise. I'm not fond of revisiting the sites of my foibles.

After I dropped off my résumé, I took a little time to reflect. All in all, I couldn't muster up an ounce of regret. The lie I'd told the judge had been stupid, but it got me out of a ticket. The one I'd told Mike MacMurtry had landed me a new job. But don't think I felt good either. At best, I was intensely ambivalent. Conflicted. I named my companions Hope and Shame.

Mostly I was conflicted because I did plan to see Dylan tonight. My friends would be up for an impromptu concert. We all liked hearing local live music, and there weren't any movies that couldn't wait. As long as they never found out Dylan was married, I was safe. Because, while I could deal with my own personal guilt-fest, I couldn't handle the well-meaning counsel they would heap upon me.

This is the part where I tell you about Jane and Luma. I hate describing people, so I'll just tell you how they talk about themselves. The ad Jane took out on Yahoo! Singles describes her as five-foot-eight (in heels) with a healthy build. She does work out twice a week, but she also loves chocolate, which means I wouldn't describe her as slender. She's that sexy bitch men flock to when she's wearing the right kind of clothes. In a lot of things, she looks kind of dumpy, but I don't have to tell her that because she knows. She's never bought anything without trying it on first, and I've never lied to her about my opinion of her proposed outfit.

Luma describes herself as the "hot Egyptian chick who really likes black men." She says it's true about not being able to go back. If I ever get the chance to find out, she assures me I should take it. Luma is lucky if she's five feet tall, even wearing shoes. She's the only person I know who makes me feel tall. Next to us, Jane's longer legs and curvier figure do stand out.

I don't often lie to either of my friends, but I did tell them many lies when we were just acquaintances. You're thinking that lying alienates people and makes them think they can't trust you. That's not always true. People generally expect others to lie to them, especially if they don't know them well—either that, or I have a knack for finding the cynics.

Jane and Luma have been around me long enough to know when I tend to lie and to whom I usually do it. They help by not putting me in situations that will lead to fabrication. We've had some frank discussions about my problem, and I can't say they understand why I do it—*I* don't understand why I do it—but they love me and are there for me when I need them.

Later that evening, I met them at Jane's apartment. She's in grad school at Detroit College of Law, which means she lives the closest to downtown Detroit. I like Detroit. It gets a bad rap for crime, drugs, and prostitution, some of which is deserved, but it's a much nicer place than most people imagine. The waterfront is gorgeous, and many of the public areas have undergone a renaissance. The area where Jane lives is about halfway refurbished. It isn't run down, but it isn't safe to wander the streets too much at night if you're alone.

Parking is where you really get screwed. Before all the flipping casinos went in downtown, parking was cheap and easy. Now it costs twenty dollars to park in an unsupervised lot. I wish I'd bought land way back when so I could hang out and make massive money letting people put their cars on it while I sit in a lawn chair for a few peak hours.

But back to Jane's apartment. It's large, nearly twice as large as mine, and her rent is about half as much. My suburban place is closer to where I worked at Pritchett Freight Services. *I wonder where Mr. Hanover's company is located? He gave me an address in Royal Oak for training. That's going to be a hell of a drive from Troy every day. Linear distance aside, the traffic is murder.*

Jane redecorated when she moved in, something I never realized you could do with a rented space, but she reasoned that Thomas Jefferson used to do it, so why not her? She'd painted various colors on the walls, some of which I liked and some of which I didn't comment on. Her furniture was just as colorful.

She'd covered the worn carpet with huge area rugs, which hid most of the boring beige, though a bit of bland might have helped tone down some of her decor. I wasn't sure how she slept at night with the glare of reds, greens, yellows, and blues pulsing at her in the dark. I know she probably couldn't see them with the lights off, but she knew they were there, and that was enough for me to never sleep over at her house.

Tonight I'd volunteered to be the designated driver. If Luma and Jane were drunk, they'd be less likely to ask questions that might lead to a discovery of Dylan's marital status. If they were really drunk, they might not remember anything even if they did ask.

Dishonesty comes in so many exciting colors, doesn't it?

Luma and I were checking our supplies and tucking our driver's licenses into our bras when Jane emerged from the bathroom. She'd been fixing her makeup after a long day of work and school. Luma was currently unemployed. She'd moved back in with her parents after college, and nobody there thought it imperative she get a job. Her mother, from what I could tell, painted terra cotta flowerpots. Her father was a free spirit who smoked a lot of weed and gave gentle, positive encouragement to everybody. Luma was the youngest of her brothers and sisters, and I think her parents didn't really want to see her fly the coop.

In the seven years I'd known Luma, I'd never heard a tale of her father losing his temper. Or getting up from whatever chair he was in. How he stayed so skinny, I have no clue. Sometimes I hate men for that reason.

We headed out to our first destination of the evening: Greektown for dinner. That meant we ordered *gyros* because we knew how to pronounce it correctly. Plus, we thought it was a fun word to say. I think we said it so much, we annoyed our waiter. No matter. We were having fun, and nobody else mattered.

Over appetizers, Jane leaned closer and nailed me with one of those sympathetic looks she likes to give when she hears bad news. She closed her hand over mine. "I heard you lost your job."

I bit my lip. I hadn't told anybody but my mom and John. I guessed at the culprit. "When did my mom tell you?"

"Today. She said you'd been out of sorts all week." She squeezed my hand once more and let go. She knows when not to overdo the physical affection.

Luma's eyes went wide. "Oh, no. Lacey, what happened?"

"Pritchett was getting ready to sell the company. I knew my days were numbered." I haven't been that torn up about losing my job.

Luma launched herself around the corner of the table and hugged me. She did not recognize public boundaries for affection. "I'm so sorry, Lacey. Is there anything I can do?"

There wasn't. "I'm fine. I knew it was coming. I have money saved up that will see me through a couple of months, and I start a new job on Monday. I'm going to be a sales rep for a liquor distributor."

Luma eased away, giving me one of those looks she gets when she thinks I'm lying. I haven't lied to her in years, but she knows I still do it regularly. "Really?"

"Really. I happened to meet the owner this afternoon, and he was so impressed that he hired me."

She nodded, satisfied with my answer. Like I said, if you ask, I always admit when I'm lying. She smoothed her skirt and sat back down, a dainty action after her spontaneous display. "So, did anything interesting happen when you were fired?"

The waiter arrived with our gyros. I waited until he'd set us up, then answered Luma's question. "Well, I sort of decided to take the situation into my own hands, and now there's a guy out there who's questioning his father's fidelity."

I presented what I considered to be an accurate accounting of the details. I left out my lunch that day and any mention of Dylan. Because it had absolutely nothing to do with me being fired.

When I finished, they stared at me in silence, neither of them particularly stunned by my revelation. Finally, Jane started giggling. Luma followed suit. I watched them laugh, clutching their stomachs as delight pealed from their mouths. It took entirely too long for them to calm down. It wasn't that funny. What I'd done had been more on the mean side.

Wiping tears from beneath her eyes, Jane faced me first. "Oh, Lacey. You're priceless. You should be in soap operas or Lifetime movies. I can see it all playing out in my head. You were probably so dramatic. How did the son react to know he had an illegitimate sister?"

Little laughs still erupted from Luma now and again, and I hoped Jane's question wouldn't send her back to Laugh Land. "I would've loved to be there for that. How come you kept this from us for a whole week?"

It hadn't been a whole week, but I was the last one qualified to correct other people's exaggerations. I shrugged. "I'm not proud of what I did. I think I verbally knocked Thomas on his ass. I felt bad for him, so I ended up quitting and storming out."

Jane snorted. "Only you would feel bad for someone who was trying to fire you."

"Yeah, Lace. I have to agree with Jane. You have to let this one go. He kind of deserved it." Luma winked and plunged into her first gyro. "Besides, you'll never see him again."

Supportive friends are wonderful for the soul.

After dinner, we wandered around, shopped a little, and bar-hopped. By the time I suggested we go listen to a new local band at The Majestic, Luma and Jane both had the giggles. I'd confessed to my worst lie this week, and I was feeling pretty good.

Mike MacMurtry caught me as I handed money to the cashier for the cover charge. His bald head still gleamed under the bright lights. He smiled as he blocked the transaction. "This one is my guest tonight."

Behind me, I felt Jane and Luma exchange glances. They smelled a juicy story. But I refused to acknowledge anything. I gave Mike a friendly/professional grin. "How are things going tonight?"

"Better. Thanks to you." He waved a hand toward my friends, gesturing for the three of us to follow him.

I waved away his compliment. "I didn't do anything." In point of fact, I'd been the one to gain the most from that conversation. To deflect anything else he might say, I introduced Jane and Luma.

Mike shook their hands. "You ladies enjoy yourselves tonight. Lacey, if you need anything, let me know."

He left us, scurrying over to answer an employee's call.

Jane cocked her head to the side. "Lace? Anything you want to tell us?"

I shrugged and pursed my lips. "It has to do with my new job. Mike's club will be one of my clients."

With that, I led them into the main room. It was packed, which made the vast chamber look much smaller. I scanned the room, automatically estimating the number of people there. It looked like Dylan was going to have a good turnout for his first performance. I hoped they took my advice about the sound mix.

Beside me, Jane and Luma followed suit, though I knew they were looking for something I wasn't.

Luma huffed out a breath full of umbrage. "Lacey, you didn't say it was an all-white event."

The music pumping through the speakers changed from AFI to Silversun Pickups. I didn't bother to look around. "An alt-rock band is performing tonight. They're playing alternative music."

She harrumphed. "Well, I guess I don't need a date for tomorrow."

Jane rolled her eyes. "Luma, you do know that refusing to date white guys is just as racist as only dating white guys, right?"

We'd discussed this before, at length, and we hadn't arrived at a consensus. Luma maintained that she couldn't help who she was attracted to. Jane liked to argue that Luma wouldn't know if she didn't try. Then Luma would bring up the fact that Jane maintained a heterosexual preference without having tried to date a woman.

I was waiting for the debate to escalate to the point where they decided to make out with one another to test the theory: Luma would be kissing a white person, and Jane would be kissing a woman. I saw it as a win-win. And I didn't care who either of them dated as long as they were happy. Though I will admit that the idea of the two of them together left me a little jealous. We'd no longer be a trio; I'd be the third wheel.

"Let it go, ladies. We're here to have fun." I spotted a high-top table near the dance floor that had just been vacated. "I see our table. We'd better snag it before somebody else does."

We made it to the table a second before another group arrived. The queen bee gave us a snotty glare.

Jane smiled, rolled her shoulders back to emphasize her breasts, and said, "You can join us. I'll even let you buy me a drink."

Luma and I exchanged glances. Pour a few drinks into Jane and she becomes flirty with just about everyone. We both wondered when she would take the dive and explore the wonderful world of women. Snotty girl and her crew sauntered away, giving Jane, I noticed, a prime view of their rear assets.

A server came over, and I threw caution to the wind and ordered a club soda. I normally wasn't one for bubbly or dry drinks. He returned with our order relatively quickly.

As she sipped her Sex on the Beach, Jane abandoned her perusal of the club's patrons and focused on me. "Lacey, I think you forgot to tell us something important."

I hadn't forgotten. As a stalling tactic, I tried to turn the conversation around. "Jane, I think you're the one holding out."

She blushed and looked away. "Damn. You're too good at that."

I wasn't good at anything; that had been a lucky strike. Still, I knew better than to let this opportunity pass. "Jane, spill. I told you my dark and dirty secret of the week."

Luma chimed in. "C'mon, Janie. If you can't tell your besties, who can you tell?"

"Well, I landed a primo internship for this fall."

We squealed. Luma and I grabbed Jane's hands. "That's wonderful." We both said lots of positive, exclamatory things, and Jane blushed harder.

"Thanks, guys. I feel sort of bad. I hadn't meant to go for that spot. I didn't think I could get it, and then the next thing I knew, they were calling me. I feel bad because Owen wanted it, and he didn't get it."

Owen was a friend of Jane's. They'd been in the same study group for two years. Leave it to Jane to feel bad about something good.

Luma snorted. "Owen's an ass. He uses you because you're brilliant. You can't feel bad for him. If he relied on you a little less, maybe he would've been actual competition."

Needless to say, Luma didn't have a high opinion of Owen. I saw him as one of those people who desperately wanted to be smarter than he was. He clung to his more intelligent friends, listened, parroted, and hoped for the best. At some point, he'd come to believe he was just as smart as everybody else. But he wasn't, and time and circumstances eventually catch up with everybody.

That delusion had led Owen to belittle Jane on more than one occasion. We didn't understand why she continued to help him study. At this news, I felt a sense of gloating vindication.

"Jane, you're a brilliant lawyer. You deserve this. Don't let Owen Glazer diminish your accomplishment."

She studied her drink, probably replaying a confrontation in her head. A frown marred her forehead and chin. "He said I could only jiggle my boobs for so long before they start sagging to my knees, and then the firm would lose interest in me."

I wanted to punch him.

Luma must have felt the same way. She narrowed her eyes to slits, and in the darkened room, she looked positively feral. "Call the son of a bitch. Invite him here. I'll come on to him in the alley out back, get him naked. Lacey will steal his clothes, and then we'll leave his ass twisting in the wind."

The plan sounded like something I'd lie about. I hoped Luma was kidding.

Jane giggled, washing away her guilt and the tension. "I love you guys."

"We love you too." Luma and Jane shared a moment of drunken awareness, then they burst with the kind of pure laughter found only in those inebriated connections. As the sober party, I felt a little left out.

"Hey, you're Lacey, right?"

I swung my attention around to see the drummer in Dylan's band. Now that I was sitting on a high-legged chair, I stood/sat face to face with her. She had the same oval face as her brother, though her jaw wasn't as square, and she also shared the dark hair and teal eyes.

I wasn't used to knowing the family members of men I dated—not that Dylan and I were dating. We'd shared two conversations in two different ladies' rooms. That wasn't romantic, and I doubted it was even hygienic. I cleared my throat and answered the woman. "Yeah."

She offered me her hand. "Daisy Day. Dylan didn't introduce us earlier. He told me about how you met."

I blushed. I've never wished so much to be drunk. Why had I thought it was a good idea to volunteer for DD duty? "It was an accident." Points to me for not stammering. I wrung my hands together, and I knew I'd be fighting the urge to wash them very soon.

Daisy laughed. "Audra and Monty thought it was hilarious."

Audra. His wife. She knew who I was. Of course she'd remember someone who spilled coffee all over her husband's lap. All of a sudden, it hit me. I was here tonight to see a married man. After all the promises I'd made to myself—after all the affirmations about how I deserved somebody honest, somebody who loved me and only me—here I was, about to dive into the same tainted pool once more.

Shame flooded my body. I wanted to cry and wash my hands. Several lies came to mind. I have a brain tumor, and I'm dying. I'm a lesbian. Anything to get me out of this situation.

I shifted uncomfortably. "Oh. I—It was an accident. I'm glad his wife isn't upset."

Daisy's brows lifted, hiding under her bangs. "Audra is *my* wife. Monty's our son."

I stared at her for a long time as her statements penetrated my thick skull. Then I thought about the second lie I'd considered, and a slow giggle trickled from me. It went on and on. Jane and Luma emerged from their love-fest to stare. Tears wet my eyelashes. Also in that manic episode was no small measure of relief. Dylan wasn't married. He'd been out with his nephew and sister-in-law.

I wasn't heading off the cliff into Bad Mistake Land. Things in my life were truly on the upswing. New job. Cute *single* guy with awesome taste in music. Night out with my best friends. My soul soared.

Chapter Five

"What's the name of the band?" Jane leaned over to ask me.

"I have no idea."

I introduced Daisy to Jane and Luma. My friends were impressed that I knew the drummer in the band, and they probably assumed I was there to support her. I didn't ask or in any way try to correct assumptions they may or may not have made.

Dylan's band opened with original music. He'd changed his clothes from earlier. They all had. Each member was now clad in a black cotton T-shirt and dark blue jeans. The three men looked scrumptious, and even behind the drum set, Daisy stood out in her V-necked baby tee.

Jane leaned closer. "If you don't know the name of the band, how did you meet them?"

I hadn't met them all. "I spilled coffee on the lead singer."

She hit me. Hard.

I winced, flinching out of her reach and rubbing my arm. "Ow. Damn it, Jane. What was that for?"

"You spilled coffee on Mr. Too-Hot-for-Words, and you're just now mentioning it? Luma and I will be torturing you for the details later.

And introductions. I concede that you have dibs on the lead singer. We'll work out who gets the keyboardist and who gets the bassist."

Dylan played lead guitar, and I was impressed at his skill. He was effectively doing two complicated things at once, and I had to wonder how that ability translated into other areas of life.

The band played another original song before launching into their version of "Endlessly, She Said." Dylan dedicated it to me, or actually to "the lovely woman with the iced latte," as he didn't use my name. I'm not sure how I feel about that gesture. I mean, I'm pretty certain the song is about the death of hope. It speaks to my soul, but it whispers dreary sentiments. This did not bode well for my prospects of exchanging my battery-powered lover for a manual one.

Meanwhile, Dylan's voice and expression seemed to mesmerize everyone in the room. I don't think anyone had expected to be swept away, but that's what he did to them. For me, those are the sweetest of experiences: the unexpectedly good ones. I went willingly, even when I realized he was singing a punked-out version of "You Give Love a Bad Name." It was almost enough to make me want to listen to Bon Jovi.

Almost.

Jane and Luma enjoyed the show tremendously. By the time Dylan introduced their last tune, my friends had sobered up.

"I'd like to thank all of you for coming out tonight. We are Kiss Me Goodnight, and this is our final song."

It started slow, with the melody kicking in after the drum established the beat. It had a catchy chorus:

> I'll lock all the doors
> And turn out the lights;
> Curl up in my arms, darling,
> And kiss me goodnight.

There was more, of course. The song told the story of lovers comfortable in the knowledge that they'd always be together. He sang it sweetly, so even though I didn't catch all the lyrics, the song still managed to penetrate my emotions.

When the band had abandoned the stage and the DJ took over the sound system again, Jane turned to me, her eyes narrowed.

"Spill it, sister. I can't believe you're holding out on us."

Luma lifted an inquiring brow, and they took turns with the interrogation.

"What's his name?"

"Dylan."

"You met when?"

"Last Friday."

"First date?"

"No."

"He ask you out?"

"No. He asked me to come see his band." I looked around. A lot of pretty girls were here. I wondered how many he had invited. Jane opened her mouth to ask the next question, but I held up my hand. "It's not a big deal. I spilled coffee on him. He asked me to come see his band play. I'm here. End of story."

They gave me the look that said they knew I wasn't telling them everything. But they also knew, from experience, that if they kept asking questions, I'd be in the bathroom until the soap dispensers ran dry.

I didn't know if Dylan would try to find me, but I wanted him to know I'd been here and I enjoyed the show. They didn't have roadies, so the band members were disassembling their own equipment. I approached the stage, but half the single women in the place had the same idea, so I stood off to the side.

Dylan worked steadily. Every time he or another band member came near the front of the stage, some groupie—I couldn't believe they already had groupies—said something to snag his attention.

When the girl next to me yelled a suggestive compliment at Dylan, he had the grace to blush as he looked over. But when he did, he spotted me and seemed to forget the woman who'd spoken. The shy smile on his face grew larger and warmer. "Lacey. Daisy told me you were here. I was hoping you'd stick around."

The girl gave me a dirty look, which I ignored. Jane and Luma had my back, and they're experts. They have older sisters. As an only child and someone who spent my childhood focused on my OCD, I was out of my depth when it came to petty dealings with women.

"Do you need help?" I asked Dylan.

He quirked a brow. "Sure. How are you at holding open doors?"

"I have a degree in that shoved in a drawer somewhere."

Jane pinched me, a warning. My statement was a joke, but I have a history of taking things to extremes.

I didn't react to the zap of pain, but I did sweep my hand up and point over my shoulder. "These are my friends, Jane and Luma. They're also great with doors."

Dylan helped us all onto the stage, which isn't as easy as it looks. But he's strong, and we all made it up there without losing our dignity.

The band worked quickly and efficiently to load the equipment into their van, which was parked in a short alley behind the bar. Dylan introduced us to the keyboardist, Levi, and the bassist, Gavin. This time they shook my hand instead of glaring.

Gavin even apologized. "Sorry if we came off as overly hostile earlier."

"That's all right. I know I overstepped my bounds. It won't happen again."

"You meant well. And you were right." He grinned, his brown eyes lit with warmth.

One thing I'll say about the band: they're hot. Every single one of them is physically attractive—tall, built, and handsome. Daisy is shorter than the guys, but still tall for a woman. And she's pretty. They looked and sounded great.

I introduced Jane and Luma to Dylan's band. Thank goodness neither of them looked at the men like they were a buffet. I liked Dylan, and now that I knew he was single, I was actually experiencing hope.

Gavin looked at Dylan and clapped Levi on the back. "We should clear out."

"No, you shouldn't." Heads swung and everybody looked at me. It was a little disorienting. I won't be going on a stage anytime soon. I swallowed. "I mean, this was your first performance. There have to be a hundred women and more than a few men hanging out in there who enjoyed your show and wouldn't mind meeting you. Mingling will help build your fan base."

I needed to shut up before somebody asked me if I was a publicist. Knowing me, I would probably answer in the affirmative. I have a major in finance with a minor in business administration. Nothing there speaks to this situation.

"Sorry. Just throwing out ideas."

Jane and Luma chuckled nervously. Jane moved closer, probably ready to drag me away if I kept going.

Levi nodded thoughtfully. "Good ideas, though. They make sense. Ladies and gentlemen, we're heading back inside."

Daisy linked her arms through Jane's and Luma's, and the three of them went first. Levi and Gavin followed.

Dylan held the door for me, which led to a hallway behind the stage. He grabbed my hand, holding me back when I would have followed everyone else through the door into the main room.

I cocked my head and gazed up at him.

"You liked the show?"

"Very much. I'd even see it again." I still think they need some backing vocals. "I especially liked the last song. That's where you took the name for your band?"

He nodded. "I wrote the song a few years ago." His eyes clouded over the tiniest bit, a combination of nostalgia and melancholy.

I was about to ask him if he was okay when he tilted his head down. The right moment had finally come. He was going to kiss me. My lips tingled with anticipation. My senses came alive, attuned to every molecule of this moment.

He pulled me against him, holding me so I could feel the hard length of his thighs (yes, *thighs*, you perv) against mine. But that wasn't enough. Taking one step forward, he moved my back against the wall. Throwing caution to the wind, I gave in to my urge to run my hands over his chest. I broke my gaze from his, putting off a moment I knew would blow away every kiss I've ever had.

You don't think I've set my hopes too high, do you?

He was hot and damp from exerting himself on stage and packing up the equipment. It's been far too long since I've reveled in having a sweaty man in my hands.

A hard, lump under his shirt caught my finger. I went to move it aside, but the clumsy part of my brain was operating at maximum capacity, and I couldn't.

As I felt it again, discerning the shape, I realized it was a ring. He was wearing a ring on a necklace. I pulled it from under his shirt and held it to the side where I could see it better.

Dylan snatched the ring from my hand and tucked it back under his shirt, regarding me with a displeased frown.

That ring was an ice bath on my libido. I was a little stunned, and a lot pissed. My instincts were dead on. "Is that a wedding ring?"

"Don't worry about it."

Son of a bitch. Don't worry about the fact that he's hiding a freaking ring? I shoved him away. "I won't."

Now he looked stunned. I had no plans to stick around and hear how his wife didn't understand him or whatever manure he was planning to spread. My hands itched with invisible soil. I tried to leave, but he grabbed my shoulders.

"Lacey, it's not what you think."

Oh, yes. I've heard this one before. I responded, turning my derision on high. "I *think* it's a wedding ring, and I'm perfectly aware of what *that* means."

He was silent, most likely wavering between guilt and uncertainty.

I wasn't going to wait until he could gather his favorite lies. "What? You're not going to tell me how your wife doesn't understand you? She doesn't support your dreams? She's cheating on you? The magic is gone? She's not into sleeping with you anymore?"

He opened and closed his mouth, but all that did was set his jaw a little more stubbornly.

So, that's how it's going to be; he's going to get defensive over his indiscretion. Well, if he's going to be a loser-jerk, I'm going to stick up for a stranger with the same bad taste in men.

"She doesn't deserve to be treated like this. Vows and fidelity mean something. If you're not into being faithful, you have no business getting married in the first place."

Crud. I think I just handed him the perfect excuse. But he actually appeared to be thinking about what I said.

"You're right, Lacey. Vows mean something, and if I was still married, I wouldn't be here with you. I'd be celebrating with her." He swallowed a lump that looked pretty painful. "Nadia died last November."

It took a minute, but my ire turned to sympathy. He'd lost his wife less than six months ago. The ring kept her close to his heart. Was this worse than if he'd still been married? I'm not sure. I don't know how to reconcile my sympathy with my relief and disappointment. I hope he's telling the truth, not because I want her to be dead, but because I desperately don't want to be the other woman again.

I stopped trying to leave. "I'm sorry for your loss."

He stuck his hands in his pockets and rocked back on his heels. "We went skiing in Utah last Thanksgiving. She was the better skier, so we separated for the afternoon. She went on a harder slope with a group of people and a guide. Apparently, she fell. Broke her neck. They said she felt no pain."

This was an entirely new situation for me. I've only rehearsed speeches, diatribes, and comebacks for situations involving still-living spouses. I didn't quite know what to say. Showing sympathy was fine, but I didn't want to overdo it. I hadn't known Nadia, and I barely knew Dylan. I waited in a way that I hoped came off as patient because I had no idea what else to do.

"Anyway, I moped around for a few months, then I decided to stop." He rubbed the back of his neck with one hand, an unconscious, soothing gesture. "She was the kind of person who took chances. I'd always wanted to be in a band, so I formed one. It seemed appropriate that she be here with me, if only in spirit."

He might not be moping, but he was still grieving; that much was apparent.

I put my hand on his arm, holding it lightly on his warm skin. "I'm sure she is here with you, so we probably shouldn't do any kissing."

He smiled and chuckled briefly, then he parked his hand on my lower back and steered me into the main room. He didn't kiss me until we parted ways, and that was only a short peck on the cheek.

My luck, it seemed, had only marginally improved.

Chapter Six

Beginning the following Monday, I found out that my job at Hanover is indeed a sales position. My responsibilities include convincing businesses to stock liquors that Hanover distributes and maintaining a good relationship with them. My department is called Client Acquisition and Services.

Basically, I sell booze to bars. Over the next two months, I traveled a lot, and I found that I have a latent gift for charming people. I channeled the skills I normally use to lie into strategies for approaching prospective clients, and I walked away from the majority of my meetings with positive results.

Mr. Hanover was so impressed that he increased my commission rate. At first I wasn't sure about the whole idea of working on commission. What if I have a bad month or get really sick? I have to work for ninety days before I'm eligible for health care. So far my job helps with rent, but not with doctor's fees. I worry about these things, so I've been extra careful to wash my hands frequently.

Dylan noticed.

You thought we parted ways after I told him he shouldn't kiss me, didn't you?

We didn't. He called me the next week—I gave him my number before we left The Majestic—and we chatted for a bit. We met for coffee several times, and I saw his band play three of their next four performances. In effect, over the next few months we became friendly. I wouldn't call us friends, per se. If I was in a car accident, he's not on the list of people I'd call. However, if I want a name for a new vibrator, "Dylan" is a good candidate.

There's always an undercurrent of tension between us that I think people expect us to act on, but we don't. Dylan isn't ready for that, and I don't want to push him. If it's going to happen, it'll happen. Otherwise, I've made a new set of buddies.

Toward the end of summer, he invited me to play softball. A few years have passed since I played softball, and I'm no longer sure about my skills. Dylan assured me that wouldn't be a problem, so I agreed to meet him at the park. When I arrived, softball season was in full swing, and hundreds of people were warming up on twelve different diamonds. I got there on time, but it was taking me a little longer than expected to find the correct field. I was scanning the mixed-gender teams when a shrill whistle caught my attention.

Dylan waved, and I hurried in his direction. He looked different today, probably because he was wearing the team uniform. The red shorts and matching shirt shattered his bad-boy image. Now he just looked cute. Daisy tossed me a spare uniform, and I changed in one of the dirtiest bathrooms I've ever seen. Public parks are not as clean as they should be.

As I tied my cleats, I surveyed the field and the benches. Women, women everywhere, as far as the eye could see. Some men were in the stands, but Dylan was the only one poised to take the field.

I bent over to stretch and heard a few murmurs of appreciation. Standing slowly, I cocked my head at Dylan. "You play in a lesbian league?"

He grinned. "It's Daisy and Audra's team. They needed a catcher."

I so badly wanted to make a pitcher/catcher joke, but it seemed out of place in this lady-filled environment. "How long have you been helping them out?"

"Just this season. Jessie, the regular catcher, had a baby. They needed someone to take over for a few months, and, according to my sister, I wasn't doing anything anyway."

He stood next to me with his hand on my lower back—friendly close, but not I-want-to-sleep-with-you close. However, I'd be lying if I denied the presence of sparks. Him still mourning his wife didn't make him any less attractive, and it also reminded me I'd finally found a man who wasn't attached.

Yet despite our budding friendship, I didn't know all that much about him. I've decided I should change that. "What do you do when you're not writing lyrics or practicing with the band?"

"Family counseling."

I looked up at him, carefully considering his career choice and his apparent attraction to me. "Is it my insanity that appeals to you?"

"You're not nuts, Lacey. You've got an OCD thing going on. Hand washing is a pretty mild manifestation."

It did explain why he both let me finish my cycle of six and was adamant that I stop afterward. John treated me the same way. "Then you must be aware that washing my hands isn't my only issue." I said that quietly, offering him a ticket off my crazy train. He was still technically at the station, and this wasn't a ride most people relished.

Whenever Jane or Luma need a break from me, they take one. I know they'll be there if I need them, but sometimes I can be a bit much. John's theory is that I act out to push people away when they're getting too close. I prefer to think of myself as somebody who occasionally needs to be alone.

Dylan tilted his head, ruminating on his response. "Everybody has issues. You haven't come close to cornering the market where that's concerned."

That was a sweet sentiment, and I wondered when the right time would be to tell him all my energy goes into controlling my urges to lie, so I don't really try to curb my hand washing.

"Your hands are looking a little raw today. Tough week?"

Some parts had been excruciating. I'd passed up more than one opportunity to deliver a juicy fabrication. And contrary to what you'd logically think, holding back doesn't make me feel better. "I'd prefer if you didn't analyze me. I've had enough of that for one lifetime."

He stroked his hand up my back. The move was both sensual and soothing—yet another of the mixed signals he liked to give. "Noted. No shrinkage. That's good. I'm not exactly an objective observer."

"No?" I thought he'd remained relatively detached throughout most of our short association. Other times, he'd been unconsciously (subconsciously?) affectionate. No, I definitely wasn't the only one on this field who had issues.

"No. Do you have plans for after the game? We all usually go out for pizza or something else that's equally healthy."

I didn't get the sense that he was asking me on a date. The fact that the entire team planned to go pointed away from that prospect. So, I took the offer at face value. "Sure. I love that kind of health food."

We lost the game, but I'd batted in one of our five runs, so I didn't feel badly about it. They'd sacrificed me to get that woman home. The other team had simply been better. Significantly better. Holding them to nine runs was difficult, so the team celebrated that they'd only lost by four. Apparently that was a victory compared to the last time they faced that team.

Dylan sat across from me at the pizzeria. The owner, who sponsored the team's uniforms, had set up a long line of tables down the center of his restaurant for them. Audra sat to my left, and Daisy took the seat next to her.

I remembered the little blonde well. Thankfully, my residual feelings of guilt had faded, and seeing her no longer triggered an urge to wash my hands. She'd been to all the Kiss Me Goodnight performances except that first one. Monty's babysitter had come down with a summer cold at the last minute, so Audra had stayed home.

They must've had a standing order because the pizza came out minutes after we sat down. The woman to my right was tall and broad-shouldered. She had a larger build, but it was solid muscle, and her long red hair was tied back in a neat ponytail. I was pretty sure her name was Missy.

She smiled at me, a friendly one that made her hazel eyes sparkle. "So, you're Dylan's new girlfriend."

Unless she'd been attuned to cues I've missed, that was a leap in logic. "We're just friends."

She lifted her brows and eyed me. "Are you playing for our team?"

I knew what she meant, but I thought it would be funnier if I pretended otherwise. "I just did. We lost."

Across the table, Dylan chuckled softly. He gave me half a grin before continuing his dissection of the game with the cute towheaded pitcher.

Missy offered a long-suffering sigh. "He always gets the prettiest ones."

I wasn't sure how to respond, so I accepted the compliment with
a cocky, flirtatious smile. Very few people have called me pretty. My
mother and John don't count. They're a little biased when it comes
to me.

After pizza, I went home to shower because Dylan wanted to
hang out some more. "Just the two of us," he said. "No nosy older
sister or her friends."

The late-August evening had grown unseasonably cool, so I threw
on a pair of jeans and a shirt with a sweetheart neckline that made
me want to play with my own girls. When Dylan knocked on my
apartment door, I grabbed a jacket and followed him to his truck.
He might eventually like watching me touch myself, but we weren't
there yet.

"Where are we going?"

He opened the passenger door for me. The scent of his aftershave
drifted on the breeze. "Will it kill you not to know?"

"No, but it might not go well for you if I'm dressed inappropriately."

He looked me up and down. His gaze stuttered twice on my
chest. Score! I did a mental fist pump.

"You look great. I mean, fine. You'll need the jacket."

A mental stutter. I was doing well tonight. After four months,
patience is becoming my strong suit where Dylan is concerned, but
I'm still hoping the mixed signals will eventually settle on the hot
side of the relationship spectrum. In the meantime, I've celebrated
the end of my dating hiatus by going out with several unmarried
men who asked me. But none of those kisses (or men) have been
memorable, and I haven't consented to any second dates.

Dylan drove for a very long time. We talked about music and
sports and what it's like to work your way through college. Like me,
he'd spent six years earning his degree.

I liked that he didn't seem to have an agenda and was easy to be
with. For the first time in my life, I opened up to somebody and told
him truthful things right off the bat. Even Jane and Luma, who'd
been my best friends since high school, had endured the morass of
my lies before I'd let them get close. Maybe the fact that Dylan put
no pressure on me worked in my favor.

He turned down a two-lane highway in the middle of nowhere, and I had no idea where we were. Absorbed in our conversation, I'd paid no attention to the scenery. He turned onto a narrow dirt road where a sign proclaimed the Highland State Recreational Trails.

"Is this open at night?"

"Probably not." He parked in a small, dirt parking lot and grabbed a blanket that had been wedged in behind the seat. "We might get chased out, but they won't arrest us. There's a flashlight in the glove box. Can you grab it?"

I got it out. Darkness descended once the truck doors were closed and the dome light faded. I searched for a switch to turn the flashlight on, but I couldn't find one. Dylan solved the problem by clicking a soft panel on the back. A strong, steady beam lit the path in front of us.

"Ah. It's one of those newfangled contraptions."

He laughed and steered me forward with a hand on my lower back. "I'm all about new technology."

I like the way he touches me. It makes me feel sexy and cherished, and that's not a feeling I experience very often. "Very manly of you."

"Well, I am a man."

Here's where I stopped myself from saying something about how I'd wondered. There's no way to make a snarky comment like that without damage to his ego. Plus, he's definitely a man. My pointy nipples could attest to that.

We followed a trail through the trees. All of a sudden, it opened up and dropped off sharply, and that freaked me out. I wasn't afraid of heights, but it was dark, and I couldn't see the bottom. Even with the flashlight, we were surrounded by inky blackness. I was the one in front, and I would have been the one pancaked at the bottom if I hadn't stopped short.

"A little warning would have been nice, Dylan. Real men warn people when they're about to plunge into an abyss."

"It's not an abyss. Watch your step, though. It'd be a nasty fall."

I threw my nastiest look over my shoulder, but I really couldn't see his face, so I surmised that he couldn't see mine either. "My ghost would haunt you forever."

He paused for a millisecond, long enough for me to regret the thoughtlessness of my joke, but then he continued. His hand tightened on my waist, and he pulled me closer. "I wouldn't let anything happen to you, Lacey."

That assurance washed over me, a quiet declaration he seemed to mean with every fiber of his being. I placed my hand on his smooth, soft cheek. It wasn't usually smooth or soft.

"I know you wouldn't."

I don't know if he was thinking about kissing me, but I was definitely having those thoughts. A heaviness hung in the air, and for a little while, I felt the palpable force of the magic between us. I hoped I wasn't the only one.

He cleared his throat. "Just a little farther ahead. It slopes down to the right."

I took the hint. He wasn't ready, and I would continue being patient. I really don't want to be with a man whose heart belongs to another woman.

The trail dropped a few feet, and flat land spread out to my left. Light from the flashlight glistened on a watery surface.

"A pond?"

"A stream. It connects two lakes."

He directed me to the bank, and that's where he spread the blanket. When he sat down and patted the space next to him, I swallowed a comment about taking him back to my place to make him scream in my bed. There was no need to traipse along dangerous paths in the dark.

I sat. He scooted back and lay down, folding his hands under his head. I set the flashlight between us. This had all the hallmarks of a seduction, but I didn't think that was his goal.

"Dylan, what are we doing here?"

"Looking at the stars. You can't really see them where we live. Too much light pollution." He turned off the flashlight, plunging us into darkness.

Then I understood. This was probably somewhere he used to come with Nadia.

I wanted to leave.

I wanted to wash my hands.

I wanted to tell him I was allergic to looking at the stars.

Careful not to make physical contact, I lay down next to him. Above me, the sky sparkled. I'd never seen this vast array without the filter of a lens or a screen. It was bitterly beautiful.

He pointed out constellations: The Big Dipper. Orion the Hunter. The Pleiades. Others whose names he knew and I can't remember. I relaxed and enjoyed what he was trying to share with me.

"Daisy used to bring me here after our parents died. We'd bring a picnic lunch and wander around for hours or sit here and talk. Sometimes we'd just sit and enjoy the silence. I was fourteen when they were killed in a car accident. She was eighteen, recently graduated from high school, and two months pregnant with Monty. Our parents never knew."

I relaxed a little, but the urge to wash my hands didn't go away.

"We didn't have any close family. She got a job and fought for custody of me. Then Monty came along, and it was the three of us. She met Audra a few months after I started college. Audra was the T.A. for one of my freshman classes. I introduced them when Daisy made me argue for a higher grade on one of my papers. She went with me to make sure I did it. I wasn't the kind of person who liked to rock the boat."

It was difficult to imagine Dylan needing somebody to force him to argue, but I guess somebody had to teach him to stand up for himself. He continued talking, and I continued listening.

"Daisy said she'd never considered dating a woman before, but the second she met Audra, she knew. It was love at first sight. Audra changed the grade on my paper without even looking at it. She blended into our family seamlessly—Monty fell for her immediately, and she became another big sister to me."

I understand losing something so profound that it leaves you feeling empty and alone, and then having someone come into your life and fill that hole. The pain never quite goes away, but it does become easier to bear. I knew exactly what he was trying to tell me, but now was not the time for me to share. This was his place, his time to reveal some of what made him tick.

He pried my hand away from the flashlight's handle—I wasn't losing that thing—and twined his fingers with mine. We stayed that way for a little while, lying next to one another, holding hands in the darkness, and watching the stars move.

"I like you, Lacey."

His soft statement rippled through the comfortable darkness.

I squeezed his hand. "I know."

He rolled toward me and up on his side. "No, I mean I really like you, Lacey."

I heard the weight of his struggle, and I felt for him. I felt for myself as well, because I'd finally met the perfect man, and he wasn't in a position to make any fairy tales come true.

A breeze lifted from the water, bringing a freshness with it that seemed to be making promises. I wanted to listen, but didn't think it wise. I'd listened to promises for years, and none of them have come true.

I wasn't sure what kind of response he was expecting, so after chewing my lip for a moment, I rolled onto my side to face him. Holding hands this way was a little awkward, but neither of us let go. His face was inches from mine, and he brushed a caress down the side of my cheek, his fingertips tickling.

I couldn't see more than his outline, which was good. This way I could imagine a sad expression on his face, with echoes of wistfulness. I don't think I could stand it if I saw something sultry or affectionate. I want to see him look at me like that, but I don't want to see it until he's actually mine.

He kissed me, brushing his lips across mine, tender and sweet. I gripped his wrist, and he cradled my head. When we both pulled back, ending the kiss, he scooted me closer to him and guided my head to the crook of his arm. I stayed like that—cuddled up to him, enjoying his body heat and his comforting, male scent—for a long, long time.

As we packed up to leave (I held the flashlight while he folded the blanket), he threw out a casual question. "Are you doing anything tomorrow afternoon?"

I happened to have plans. "Baking a cake."

In the dim glow, I saw his expression change from shy to very interested. "What kind of cake?"

"German chocolate." My mom and I make one every year on my birthday. John sits at the counter on a bar stool, mostly watching us bake and listening to us chat. Sadie curls up at his feet and nibbles on anything we drop.

"That's my favorite."

I laughed. I sensed that any kind of cake was his favorite. "Mine too. I have a weakness for coconut."

He slung the folded blanket over his shoulder and put his arm around me. It was the same pose he'd used to guide me down here, only now it was a little more familiar.

"I have a weakness for chocolate," he said. "And cake."

I wasn't going to invite him to my mother's house, not for my birthday. I sometimes invite Jane and Luma, but only for dinner. The time before that, when we do the baking and cooking, is sacred. Only my family is allowed.

"If there's any left, I'll save you a piece."

"Maybe you could bring it to watch me practice tomorrow? I wrote a new song I'd like you to hear. It needs something, and you always seem to know exactly what will make us better."

I snortled, which is a cross between a snort and a chuckle. It's not a ladylike noise, but I wasn't going to pretend to be someone I'm not.

I do critique the band's performances, and now that they know me, they take a lot of my feedback into account. Except they still ignore the part where I insist they need more vocals. "Probably needs backup singers. I don't see why Gavin and Levi can't join in. Or Daisy. She has a great voice. You guys could do a couple of duets."

"No, it's something else. And I do agree with you about the backup singer thing. I'm hoping they'll all try it in practice if you're there."

"Sorry. I'm spending the day with my mom and her husband."

We'd made it back to the narrow part of the path. He held on to me a little tighter. "Her husband? That would be your stepfather?"

I don't think I've ever mentioned my mom or John to Dylan before. We keep our conversations to larger topics like continental drift or the evolution of AFI's music.

"I don't call him that."

"You don't like him?"

"I love him," I said. "He's one of my favorite people."

"What do you call him?"

Dylan had put on his counselor hat. I wanted to knock it off his head. "John."

"Are you close with your dad?"

I stumbled. Dylan caught me, pulling my back against his front. He held me for a few seconds, as if he'd realized how uncomfortable his question was for me. Because I held the flashlight, and a basic instinct wouldn't let me release my grip, I couldn't rub my hands together to simulate washing them. I rubbed my wrist instead. It kept a gruesome flow of images from manifesting.

"He died when I was little. I didn't really know him."

For all intents and purposes, John is my father. I hate the word and all the emotional baggage that comes with it, so he never forced the issue. He never sought to adopt me because I don't want to have that association with him.

Dylan hugged me a little tighter. "I'm sorry." He lost his parents. Of course he thought he knew what I was feeling. He didn't.

"Don't be. I'm not. I have John." I'm not sorry my father is dead. I have a lot of other emotions wrapped up in that mess, but sorrow isn't one of them.

I liked that Dylan was perceptive enough not to push the issue. I talk about my father with exactly one person: John. Nobody else gets to hear my thoughts or feelings about the man who nearly destroyed my life.

Chapter Seven

rang the doorbell. If I wanted, I could've gone inside without knocking. But I didn't want to. When I moved out, I stopped using my key and treating this house like it was my home.

My mom doesn't like it, but John has assured her that it's a normal part of me asserting my independence. My mom does like when I assert my independence. For so many years, I was a little phantom clinging to her or John, hiding behind them until they forced me to stand on my own.

John answered the door, pushing open the screen and pulling me into a hearty embrace. John is a good hugger. He has a knack for finding the perfect pressure and placement of everything, and you can tell he means it. He held me for a few seconds, and then he kissed the top of my head. He's a tall man, a little on the skinny side, and he dwarfs me. I felt like a little girl again, safe and secure.

"Hey, princess. Happy birthday. Come on in. Your mother's in the shower. She just went up, so we have some time."

My mother takes epic showers. When I was about twelve, John replaced the water heater with one of those on-demand things because he was tired of the rest of us having to take cold showers all the time.

I rose to the tips of my toes and rubbed his head. As long as I've known him, John has been bald. He takes great pride in making sure his pate is nice and shiny. It matches the sparkle he gets in his eyes whenever he looks at me or my mom. I like to think I've inherited that sparkling tendency from him.

We went into the living room. I settled into an oversized recliner, and he got comfortable on the couch. This is a familiar arrangement, the one we seem to favor for our discussions.

"We haven't seen you much this summer. How are things going?"

I've been very busy with work, and I've been spending more and more time with Dylan. I told my friends and family about my job change, but I haven't said much to anyone about Dylan, mostly because there's nothing to tell. My palms suddenly became sweaty. I wiped them on my jeans. "I met someone."

"Yeah?" John kept his tone mild, though I knew he had to be dying from curiosity.

"Yeah." I didn't quite know what to say from here. John is the person who's put the most time and effort into convincing me I deserve more from men than I've been settling for.

He sat up a little straighter. "What is this young man's name?"

"Dylan Day. He's twenty-four. He's a family counselor during the week, and he's a singer in a band on the weekends."

"Married?"

I expected this question, but it still stung. I shook my head. "His wife died in a skiing accident last winter. I've met his family."

John considered the scant information I gave him. He knew it was huge for me to even mention a man I liked. He rubbed his thumb under his chin. "Is he boyfriend material?"

That was a great question. I wasn't sure I had an answer. "Not yet. He's still in mourning. We're friends. We've been hanging out some this summer. Last night, he told me he likes me."

"He likes you?" John frowned. "What's that supposed to mean?"

I hoped it meant he was closer to getting over his wife. I shrugged. "I think it means he likes me. I haven't told a lie in four months."

Maybe that was a manipulative thing to say, but I wasn't sure I wanted to answer many more questions about Dylan.

John took the bait. It was kind of hard for him to ignore. He sat forward. "Four months? That's amazing, princess. I'm very proud of you."

"Thank you." I might have blushed a little under his praise. John is one of the few people whose opinion matters to me.

"Are you taking meds?"

I shook my head. I'd gone several rounds with antidepressants, which were supposed to treat my condition but didn't. John has done a lot of cognitive behavior therapy with me, and that seems to work the best. I should also mention that he did very much try to help me with my root cause. Unlike many people who suffer from OCD, I have a triggering event.

But we won't get into that now.

My mom came into the living room just then. She gave me a hug and kissed my cheek a dozen times. "I think I overheard you say you haven't lied in four months. Is that true?"

Genevieve Zimmerman is the prettiest mother in the world, though I might be a little biased. She's tall and willowy. Her long curly hair is a beautiful shade of auburn, and she has deep brown eyes that positively glow. She's also a very intelligent woman. She knows the right questions to ask. To be fair, I'm sure John was getting ready to work that question into the conversation. They both know I'll tell them the truth when asked directly.

"It's true." I gave her the date of my last incident, and then I felt obligated to tell her about the court appearance. The object of said appearance chose that moment to jump up on John's lap.

Sadie is a smaller dog. She weighs in at about thirty pounds, so she's the perfect size for John's lap. Her short black fur is mottled with browns, and she has some white on her chest. She is thoroughly a mutt.

He stroked her head and patted her flank. "Hey, baby girl. I hear you've been causing some trouble."

I couldn't let Sadie take the blame. "I'm the one who let her off her leash. She runs so much faster than me, and it makes her so happy."

John grinned and let out an aggravated sigh. "I'm not sure it would do any good to say you should've told us. We would've gone with you."

They would've kept me honest, is what he means. I blushed, still both proud and ashamed of my subterfuge. "I know."

"But the important thing," my mother interjected, "is that it's the last lie she's told." She kissed my cheek again and patted my hand. "You've come so far, sweetheart."

I looked down at her hand on mine, and warmth washed through me. It was good to be home. "Come on, Mom. That cake isn't going to make itself."

Jane and Luma dropped by at five to join us for dinner. I like this quiet birthday tradition. Over the years, I've celebrated in the usual ways—everything from big productions at the Pools and Fitness center to bounce houses to sleepovers—but I prefer a small dinner with those I love.

And my mother's German chocolate cake recipe is to die for. I do not use that term lightly, and I know you're wishing you were here with us for real.

It was a good dinner, even though Mom had a lot of questions about Dylan. I answered them the best I could, and I kept reminding her that we weren't dating and I didn't know him all that well. Jane and Luma added liberal doses of their opinions—they'd liked Dylan on the several occasions when we'd all hung out together.

I didn't get home until several hours after Dylan's practice was over. Right after I chucked my bra into the hamper and slipped into my sleep pants, my buzzer went off. I live in one of these apartment buildings with a security door and an intercom. In theory, I could push one button to talk to my visitor and another to let my visitor inside. In reality, there was a problem with the electrical system and pushing either of the buttons did nothing.

I frowned as I trudged out of my apartment, down a flight of stairs, and over to the building's heavy metal door. The only person who ever stopped by unannounced was John, and he'd been yawning up a storm by the time I left at eight.

When I pulled it open, Dylan filled the doorway. He wore a teal shirt that worked with the light coming at him to make his eyes glow. My surprise must have shown on my face because he shifted nervously and shoved the fingers of his right hand into his jeans' pocket.

He offered me a half smile. "Hey."

I wasn't unhappy to see him, but I couldn't think of a reason he'd show up unannounced. I preferred announced visits. That generally gave me enough time to get dressed or put on a bra. I crossed my arms over my chest, hoping nothing had gotten embarrassingly pointy.

"Hi." Then it hit me. "We ate all the cake." I felt a little sorry, but I hadn't promised I would save him some.

He offered a short, nervous laugh. "That's not why I'm here."

It didn't seem like he was going to say anything substantive in the doorway, so I stepped back and inclined my head toward the stairs. "Want to come up?"

"Sure. If you aren't busy."

I gave a long-suffering sigh. "I don't know. I had an exciting evening of watching TV planned."

When he laughed this time, he sounded a lot less nervous. "Don't let me stop you."

I led him up into my apartment and locked the door behind us. Though he'd been to my building several times, I'd always come out to meet him. This was the first time he'd been inside my place.

It's a small apartment. One person doesn't require a lot of room, and I like the fact that I can clean the entire thing in one afternoon. The front door opens directly into a small dining area that's separated from the kitchen by virtue of a short counter. I have a little table pushed up against the wall, but it's piled high with file folders and unopened mail.

My laptop sat on the counter. At least that surface was clear.

Through the dining room, the space opens up to reveal my living room, which is filled with hand-me-down furniture. It's in good repair, but nothing in my apartment is new. To the left of the dining room, a hallway leads to the bathroom and my bedroom. One day, I hope to have Dylan in there.

I swept my hand toward the sofa, and realized it was piled with throw pillows and laundry. I scurried over and threw the clean clothes back into the basket.

"Sorry. I wasn't expecting company."

"That's okay." He grinned as he plopped down, and I knew he had to be thinking about my OCD and the fact that it apparently didn't extend to my living space.

I chucked the basket into my bedroom.

When I came back, he patted the cushion next to him. "Come here. I want you to hear this." He held an earbud in his outstretched hand.

I peered at it doubtfully. I don't have a phobia about germs, but I hate having those things in my ears. "I have my own."

No argument from him. He plugged my headphones into his iPod and touched the screen. Music filled my ears, and I recognized the song immediately. "You recorded 'Kiss Me Goodnight.' Wow. This is huge."

I listened to the entire thing. Something about hearing the song in its recorded form made me realize exactly how good they were. My crush on Dylan hadn't colored my perception of their music. They had real talent.

When the song ended, I unplugged my headphones and set them on an end table. "That sounds incredible. You layered in the backing vocals."

"Yeah. Well, this incredibly awesome woman kept telling me we needed them. Turns out she was right." He slid his iPod into his pocket and leaned back against the sofa. "I had to do them, though. I can't get anybody else to sing."

"But now that they've heard the song, how can they argue?"

"Levi has zero vocal talent. Gavin doesn't think he can sing and play. Daisy won't even discuss the idea."

Daisy was a stubborn potato. I could see he wouldn't get far by arguing with her. But Levi and Gavin had no excuse. "You'll have to practice it that way. It makes a difference."

"I know. I was hoping you might consider singing backup."

My voice is okay for background noise, but there's no way in hell I would ever get on a stage. I shook my head. "I'm not a performer. I'm happy to support you by watching and telling everyone I meet how wonderful your band is. I'll even wear a T-shirt. But that's all."

He put on all the charm in his arsenal, which was considerable, and leaned closer. "Can I seduce you into doing it?"

I shook my head and delivered my refusal in my gravest tone. "Seducing me would only get you laid."

I'm not sure what kind of reaction I expected, but from the look in his eyes, he was no longer thinking about convincing me to sing backup. The distance between us vanished, and his lips claimed mine. It was a different kiss from last night. It wasn't slow, but it wasn't impulsive or desperate either.

It was calm and affectionate, an insistent exploration. He cupped my head in his hands, ran his fingers through my hair. He touched my cheeks and my eyebrows. He traced his thumb along the edge of my lower lip.

I've never felt so drugged. Time seemed to slow down and speed up. I lost all sense of the world. At that moment, he could have seduced me.

He didn't.

After an eternity sped by, he ended the kiss. He leaned against the sofa and put his arm around me, pulling me back with him. He picked up the TV remote and surfed the channels with me snuggled against his side.

"Tell me something about you, Lacey." His scratchy command powered over those coming from the television, laying waste to any products I might have considered buying.

As a rule, I don't talk about myself too much. Of course, by writing this, I'm totally breaking that rule. But I don't have much practice opening up. Under the weight of his arm, I gave a miniscule shrug as I searched for something of substance that wasn't too revealing. "I was a band nerd through middle and high school."

He played with a ringlet of my hair. "I bet you were in the goth section."

I tilted my head to see him. "Were you?"

"Nope. I played baseball in the summer and basketball in the winter. My musical activities were all extracurricular. I learned to play guitar my senior year because a girl I had a crush on thought guitar players were hot."

I considered this. Our paths wouldn't have crossed in high school. "What was the first song you learned?"

I expected something simple, like a nursery rhyme. That's how I started out. This time, his shoulders rose and fell. "'Endlessly, She Said.' Turns out the girl wasn't into AFI. That killed it for me." He shifted so he could sprawl the length of the sofa with me tucked into his side. "Tell me a little about John. How old were you when you met him?"

I looked up at him again, checking to make sure he wasn't analyzing me. His attention seemed to be on a commercial for a vacuum cleaner. I decided to take a gamble. "Six. He was my counselor. By the time I was eight, he'd married my mother. I guess having a crazy kid wasn't a deal breaker for him."

Dylan stroked my hair. "That had to be confusing for you. My parents were so in love with each other. I can't imagine what it would be like to have a stepparent."

Relating, that's what he's doing. Not fishing. I can handle this. Though my hands tingled because of the topic, the urge to wash them hadn't become pressing. "My parents' relationship was over before it began. I never saw them do anything but tolerate one another. My mom and John are madly in love." I think my father was in love with my stepmother, but I couldn't be sure. That was too long ago for those memories to be reliable. They were tainted anyway, so I double-checked the locks on the door to those recollections and added another layer of reinforcement.

Dylan dropped that line of inquiry, and I was thankful. Too much pushing would have unintended consequences. He stroked a casual caress over my hair and down my arm. If we spoke again that night, neither of us said anything significant. I think it's what we didn't say that's important.

Chapter Eight

The next morning, I woke up clutching my extra pillow to my chest. Dylan had left sometime around midnight. Before that, I'd fallen asleep on his shoulder, and I was pretty sure he'd drifted off as well. He awakened me and told me to lock the door behind him and go to bed.

My job as a sales representative meant I worked mostly in the afternoon. So I slept in, showered, and was dressed by eleven. Not bad. I had some paperwork to take care of before a meeting with a potential vendor. I wanted to have my homework done before I got there. It always impresses clients when I know a ton about their business without them having to tell me.

I checked in with the office, confirmed my schedule, and had lunch. My buzzer rang right about the time I finished off my bowl of mac and cheese. Like last night, I wasn't expecting anybody. Unlike last night, I now had an idea about who would come to my apartment unannounced.

This time I checked the mirror before I went downstairs to let in my gentleman caller. I opened the door, and a saucy greeting died on my lips.

The man at my door was not Dylan. He was about the same height, but he had a slimmer build (though Dylan was pretty thin), light brown hair that curled at the ends, and hazel eyes. Dressed in a suit, he stood out in this area. Neighbors walking their dogs took a second look at him, then at me, probably speculating as to what kind of trouble I was in.

I spent a moment trying to place him, and then I remembered the goatee. "Mr. Pritchett?"

I hadn't thought of him since the beginning of summer. A left-over bit of guilt pinged off the lower section of my spinal cord and radiated down my legs.

"Hi, Lacey. Can we talk?"

I shook my head. I didn't want to have another conversation with Boss Junior. The past four months had gone pretty well where my worst compulsion was concerned. Now he was like a drug dealer who came to my door because I'd stopped coming to see him. *Please don't offer me any free samples.*

I offered a polite smile. "I have another job."

With that, I tried to close the door, but he put his hand out and halted the momentum. He was stronger than he looked. I wondered what was going on behind his expensive suit.

He came closer, and I caught the spicy edge of his scent. With his face less than a foot from mine, I suddenly became aware of him as a man: a handsome, commanding presence that made my girly bits tingle. Four months ago, I'd dismissed him outright. Even though I had a serious crush on Dylan, today I couldn't seem to look away from Junior's penetrating hazel gaze. Hopefully he hadn't come over to murder me.

"I'm not here to offer you a job. The company has been dismantled and sold. My father passed away this morning, and I came to ask you about some of the things you said the last time we met."

My face flamed, and sympathy surged through me. "I didn't mean it. I was upset, and that was a cruel thing to say. I'm sorry for your loss, and I'm sorry I maligned you and your father. None of it was true."

His lips set in a hard line. He hovered over me like a dark cloud with a lightning bolt poised and pointed in my direction. "This isn't a conversation I want to have in a hallway. Is there somewhere private we can meet to discuss this?"

"There's nothing to discuss. I lied to you, and now I've apologized. I recognize that might be too little, too late, but it's the best I can offer." I didn't want to invite him inside. What if he wanted revenge and I end up a Lacey ghost in a pool of blood?

He stepped back, probably realizing how threatening he appeared. He let go of the door and ran his hand through his hair, leaving it ruffled and adding a heaping dose of charm to his demeanor. "I'm not looking for an apology. My father did mess around on his wives. My mom was his third. They divorced when I was five, and we moved to Connecticut. I have two older half-sisters and a half-brother, and I heard rumors about a younger half-brother, but they turned out not to be true. Believe me when I say your accusations didn't upset me. They just surprised me. That's all."

He wasn't the only one suffering from shock. As I said before, I hadn't pictured the late Mr. Pritchett as a womanizer. He hadn't seemed like one of those creepy old leeches. He'd been nice to me, a bit fatherly. I'd liked him.

I'm not sure what about Thomas's speech got to me, but I let him in. I cleared a corner of my dining table and offered him a seat. "Can I get you something to drink? I have orange juice, water, or I could make coffee."

He shook his head. "I don't want to put you to any trouble. I brought you something." From his inside jacket pocket, he extracted a long, slim plastic bag.

I stared at it, recognizing the swab stick and sterile container from several police dramas I've watched. I sat across from him and scooted some papers out of my way. "Thomas, I lied to you. I swear your father is not my father. I knew my father. He died when I was six."

He shook his head. "I don't believe that. I think you're afraid. I came to tell you not to be. If this test comes back positive, his estate owes you your fair share."

I felt like an ass. I've lied plenty in my time, and some of the consequences haven't been pleasant, but this is the first time I've felt like I went too far. Lying to a judge might seem like big potatoes, but it wasn't personal. This was personal for Thomas.

The directions for obtaining the sample were easy to follow. I took the scraper out of the vial. "This is a waste of time and money."

"It's my money, and it's not taking too much time." He took a padded envelope from another pocket. It had a laboratory address filled in, and the postage had been prepaid. "If it comes back negative, no harm done. If it comes back positive, you'll be able to claim part of his estate."

I didn't want to claim part of his estate. Shaking my head, I regarded him somberly. I've lied with ease for so many years, and now I'm telling the truth and having trouble convincing Thomas of that. Maybe if I come clean about my sordid past?

"Thomas, I lie. I've told lies since I was a little girl. It's a compulsion, something I can't stop. I do it when I'm stressed or anxious." I wrung my hands together and let that washing motion bring me a little comfort. "I took a job in payroll because it seemed like it would be unexciting and not stressful. And it was until you came and started firing people. I knew the moment Alec said you'd been looking for me that you were going to fire me. I needed that job."

He held up a hand. "I hadn't planned to fire you that day. It was my intention to get into your records to figure out whether I should close completely or pare down costs and sell."

Either way, I would have eventually been out of a job.

"When you got hysterical, I wasn't sure how to handle the situation. My father was dying, and I was stuck in a place far from home. I don't have family, not really, and I don't have friends here. I just wanted to finish and get back to Connecticut."

He'd managed his confusion nicely. I nodded. "So, you fired me and availed yourself of the files. Did you fire everybody?"

He shook his head. "After you stormed out, word got around. Within a week, over half the staff was gone. I sold it." Lifting his hand, he indicated the swab stick I held. "If you're my sister, you're entitled to your portion. And that wasn't Dad's only holding. He liquidated most of his assets years ago. I don't know why he held on to the distribution center so long."

If he'd known he was coming to the end of his life, he'd probably wanted to simplify, but he hadn't wanted to bow out of the game entirely. That did explain why such a wealthy man would show up at one lowly company once or twice each week. He'd wanted to remain connected to something.

I put the DNA test kit down. "I'm not your sister."

"You said you're a liar. How do I know you're telling the truth?" His smile was encouraging and ironic. Did he find my confession funny? I revealed something to him that I've only relayed to a limited number of people. His lack of reaction was anticlimactic. Jane had cried. Luma hadn't talked to me for three days. Thomas seemed to note the fact and move on.

I couldn't afford to lie about this. "If you ask me if I'm telling the truth, I'll give you an honest answer."

He stroked the beard part of his goatee. "A DNA test will give a definitive answer. Anything you say won't matter."

I think the last time we met I'd been too overwrought and focused on my melodramatic lie to notice that Thomas was a truly frustrating man. For some reason, that insight made him even more attractive.

Setting down the test kit with an authoritative finality, I rose from my seat and took the two steps required to put me next to his chair. "Thomas, I am not your sister. We are not related. If we were, I wouldn't do this."

Splaying my fingers wide, I ran them across his cheeks and into his hair. It was short around the ears and longer on top, so my fingers didn't disappear into anything thick or luxurious, but what I did encounter was soft.

He looked at me, curiosity morphing to shock. His hazel eyes smoldered with danger. "Lacey—"

Before he could protest, I touched my lips to his. They were silky and firm, and his goatee tickled against my face. I'd never kissed a man with facial hair before, and I have to admit I wasn't expecting much. Wow, was I pleasantly surprised.

With a soft moan, I deepened my foray. Thomas took over, and tingles beat a path all the way to my toes. When I started this, I hadn't thought it would be anything special.

Our kiss ended slowly, and I could tell he was as reluctant to part ways as I was. Bits of clouds floated around my head, and something firm pressed against my bottom. I looked up and realized Thomas had switched our positions.

He loomed over me, a handsome specter in an expensive suit, and his expression was grim. "Get the DNA test done, Lacey."

That jarred me back to reality. "Thomas, I swear—"

"I know what you said, but I can't get the image of you storming out of your office out of my memory. The next time I kiss you, I want there to be no doubts in my mind."

He picked up a pencil and wrote on a file folder. "This is my cell number. I'll be expecting a call in two weeks."

With that, he left my apartment. I sat at the table for a long time, staring at the ten digits he'd scrawled on a folder that contained account information for The Majestic, my first client.

What did he mean by "next time"? He was planning to see me again if the test proved I wasn't his half-sister? Did getting the test done mean I wanted to see Thomas again? What about Dylan? What if he decided he was over Nadia and wanted me?

What does it say about me that I'm willing to sit here like a doormat and wait?

I can't remember ever being this confused in my life. In this foggy state, I scraped the inside of my cheek and dropped the envelope into a mailbox on my way to work.

What the heck? The least I could do was to put his mind at ease.

Chapter Nine

You're probably wondering what happened next between Dylan and me. I could put in some killer montage here, showing us hanging out at clubs and playing more softball and walking in the park and talking for hours. Those things definitely happened. At the end of it, I could show us kissing in the moonlight, then cut to us silhouetted in a bedroom. Dylan could lift my shirt over my head...I could fade to black or kiss and tell...

I'd like to be able to say he'd experienced some closure, and that he'd at least kissed me again, but I can't. Well, I could, but I'd be lying. I don't mind lying (as you know), but telling that one would just make me sad. The fantasies, though...Ahh...I'm blushing.

Over the next month, Dylan and I continued in the same manner that has marked the majority of our interactions. It was as if he'd never taken me to a stream at night, held my hand on the bank, and told me he liked me. I now had five original Kiss Me Goodnight songs on my iPod, but Dylan hadn't tried to kiss me again, not even on the cheek.

A large manila envelope with a return address from a lab in Ann Arbor lay buried beneath file folders on my table. I hadn't opened it, and I hadn't texted Thomas. Just thinking about him confused me. I wanted to kiss him again. I wanted to spend more time with the man who seemed to just accept the compulsive lying problem I was trying to overcome. Or maybe he hadn't believed me at all. The men in my life definitely bewilder me. Perhaps if Dylan would stop straddling the fence and move forward with whatever is or isn't going on between us, I'd be able to clarify what and who I want a little better.

Even my dreams couldn't make up their minds. Both men starred in my nighttime soap operas, sometimes taking turns and sometimes morphing into one another in the middle of the good parts. I also spent a lot of time with Simon and Jared. Davey has to be feeling neglected, but I can't look at him without thinking about Dylan, and that tends to shove me off the Cliffs of Insanity. I haven't lied in five months now, but the skin on my hands is perpetually red.

Dylan gave me a gift bag with some cream and gloves to wear at night. He didn't comment, but sometimes when he sees me heading to the bathroom, he blocks my path or shakes his head in warning. I think he's getting to the point where he might take drastic measures to stop me. If I want him to think of me as date material, I seriously need to stop washing my hands so often. This triggers his therapist instincts instead of appealing to his baser ones. I want the base ones. I want to unleash the guy who shoved me against a wall after his first performance and almost kissed me.

Today I have a meeting with the manager of The State Theater. They have frequent concerts and club nights, and they attract bigger names. This is the venue where I once saw AFI. Several years have passed, but my brain replays snippets of that night every now and again.

Mr. Hanover hasn't tried to land this contract because it's well known that the manager, Brooke Dorsey, has used the same liquor distributor since she took over eight years ago. I don't know what their deal is, but when I called to beg for a meeting, she agreed. Undertones of impatience and irritation had come through in her voice, but I didn't take it personally. That just meant I need to find out how to win her over. At least she agreed to see me.

The State Theater became part of the Live Nation franchise a few years ago, and also became The Fillmore. I use their new name with reluctance. Their Renaissance Revival architecture is being restored, and it's gorgeous. It looks better every time I visit. But to me, this place will always be The State Theater. Perhaps it's legal to rename historic landmarks, but I reject changes I don't like. Likewise, Comerica Park will always be Tiger Stadium to me. (So what if it's a completely different stadium in a different location?) I hope I don't slip up and call The Fillmore by the wrong name during my meeting with Brooke.

The lobby was empty. I've become used to seeing places like this with nobody around, as daily operations are normally quiet. If a band is scheduled to play, they generally don't show up until early evening. Now that Kiss Me Goodnight has five months of performances under their belts, they no longer show up twelve hours early to set up and practice.

I meandered toward the back of the lobby, admiring the progress they've made on the restorations. Filigree and ornate decorations lent weight to the history of this expansive space. I could close my eyes and hear an orchestra tuning and the rustle of ladies' skirts as they rushed to find their seats.

Without signs pointing the way and nobody to direct me, I wandered the place, looking for a hallway that might take me to the offices. The sound of voices eventually drew me to the third level, where conversation drifted out an open door.

Please keep in mind that this transcript is highly paraphrased. There may have been some colorful language used, and I chose not to put it here. Call me a prude. Go ahead.

Male Voice One: We don't need an opener.

Female Voice: People are expecting an opening band. We promoted it that way.

Male Voice One: They cancelled. Nothing we can do about it. Besides, it's the headliner's job to book an opener.

Male Voice Two: There are plenty of local acts who would jump at this.

Female Voice: Yeah, but the people coming tonight expect more than local talent. Walk the Moon has a national following. We can't replace their opening act with some unknown alternative band.

Male Voice Two: My cousin's band—

Male Voice One: Knows five songs.

Male Voice Two: You gotta listen to this.

As he finished speaking, a song started. I listened. The band was okay. They had a female lead who didn't quite hit all the notes and a mix that was too guitar-heavy. The lead guitar overwhelmed the vocals. I wondered if that was a common mistake for newer bands.

After the song stopped, they went back to arguing. I paused in the hallway, uncertain as to whether or not it would hurt my cause to interrupt their problem-solving session to ask for directions to the manager's office. I took a deep breath and prepared to knock on the open door.

When I looked inside, everybody's backs were turned to me, and with my fist poised, I stalled. I could see the iPod dock on a table just inside. Though I hadn't planned to see a concert this evening, I did enjoy the two songs I'd heard from Walk the Moon. They had a throwback sound that brought to mind the best of the eighties mixed with modern rock.

Plus, fans of that band were the kind of people who would like Kiss Me Goodnight's sound. I extracted my iPod from my pocket, amazed that they hadn't heard me yet. They were talking about a few of the local acts. It looked like they were leaning in that direction.

I pulled their device from the dock and put mine on in its place; Kiss Me Goodnight's self-titled song cued up. I waited, but nobody looked in my direction. Taking a deep breath, I pressed play.

Daisy's drums and Levi's keyboards started slow. Now the two men and the woman turned toward the speaker. I smiled as Dylan's haunting vocals filled the silence.

Male Voice One stood when he finally saw me. "Excuse me. We're having a meeting here." He came toward me, a menacing expression on his face.

He was attractive — tall, dark, and handsome, broad shoulders, mocha skin. Luma would be swooning. He was tempting, but I managed to hold myself together.

Female Voice said, "Wait. I kinda like this song."

And just like that, I landed Kiss Me Goodnight an opening gig for Walk the Moon.

I wish.

Truthfully, they argued among themselves for a few more minutes. But by the time the next song came on, I was getting questions about the band and their ability to fill a thirty-minute slot.

Male Voice Two introduced himself. He was smallish and pasty, the type of man who went into accounting and finance. Because that's my degree, I know exactly what I'm talking about.

"I'm Harold Watkins, financial manager for The Fillmore. Are you authorized to negotiate on behalf of the band?"

I shook his hand. "Lacey Hallem. I'm their manager."

And just like that, five months of not lying came to a screeching halt. I could blame Harold for mentioning the word *manager*, but I think we all know by now how I respond to anxiety. I'd done something ballsy, and now I had to ride this out.

Female Voice rose and shook my hand. She had a much tighter grip than Harold. "Brooke Dorsey. I thought you were coming here to sell me beer."

I gave her a friendly, easy smile. It was totally fake. Things were buzzing around inside my stomach that made me queasy. "I'm here to sell you the finest liquors, but when I overheard your problem, I felt compelled to offer a solution."

At least that part was honest. I'm all about the compulsions.

Male Voice One also shook my hand, though rather reluctantly. "Darnell Long. I handle promotions." His hand enveloped mine. He had a great grip, and his sensual lips radiated sin. Luma was going to die if I ever had a chance to introduce them.

"Kiss Me Goodnight can deliver a thirty-minute set of original music, or a forty-minute set that includes some cover songs. They like to play a few just to give audiences something familiar. It helps people connect with them and their music."

Darnell narrowed his eyes. "Thirty minutes with two covers. They'll be one of two opening acts. Let's talk equipment and compensation."

An hour later, I had a one-night contract for Kiss Me Goodnight. It listed me as their manager and included language for my six-percent take. I wasn't sure how the band would react to that part, and I knew I had to go to them with my tail between my legs.

I did not manage to land a liquor contract. Brooke had sighed and shook her head when we finally got to that topic. "My brother-in-law has that contract. I can entertain a bid, but to be honest, I won't seriously consider it. We're getting one hell of a deal."

No matter how much I insisted she talk numbers with me, she was only interested in discussing the band. And in her shoes, I might have acted the same way. Her problem was snaring an opening act, not plying patrons with drinks. But, either way, I had a foot in the door. And I can't say I pushed the issue very hard either. Suddenly I was distracted by their need for an opening act as well. If this was going to happen for KMG, I needed to get to them right away so they could get themselves together. I could have called, but this was the kind of news that should be delivered in person.

Dylan was out when I stopped by the house. After his wife's death, he'd moved back in with Daisy and Audra, occupying his old bedroom. I hadn't been up there, but I knew Audra had recently helped him repaint it, so the room probably no longer hinted at the teenaged boy who'd once occupied it. Daisy answered the door in jeans and a button-down white shirt. I could tell she was ready to leave for her waitressing job, and from the expression on her face, she was not thrilled by that prospect.

"Daisy, I need you to get the band together right now. I have important news."

She tilted her head and gave me an odd look. "What's going on?"

"I want to tell all of you guys together."

Shaking her head, she pushed the door wide and invited me in. "That's not going to happen. Dylan took Monty to the movies. Levi is out to dinner with his girlfriend's parents. Gavin has a date."

I closed the door behind me, sealing in the cooler air as I followed her toward the kitchen. She packed plastic containers into a lunch bag, and I freaked out a little. Wringing my hands together, I begged. "Daisy, I have a contract for you guys to open for Walk the Moon at The Fillmore tonight, but you have to be there in three hours."

She froze. "You're shitting me."

"No. You're entirely too big for that. Ouch. There's a catch, but it's a paying gig in front of three thousand people. There's no time to get CDs made, but I know you have a box of shirts in the basement." It wasn't an ideal marketing situation, but it was better than nothing. Opportunities like this did not grow on trees, and Daisy knew it.

"Lacey…"

I heard the hope in her voice. "Call the guys. You need this."

She reached for her cell. "Audra is teaching a late class tonight. Can you watch Monty until she gets home?"

"I got him and Audra tickets to the concert." I hoped I wasn't overstepping my bounds, but if I was, that would be among the lesser offenses they'd nail me for. I'd also picked up tickets for Luma and Jane. The three of us had made plans to meet for dinner anyway.

She nodded, but when she spoke, it was to the person on the phone. "Dylan, get your skinny ass home. We got us a gig tonight."

Daisy managed to collect all the band members, and the concert went well. Monty stuck to my side like glue, probably because I got to go backstage, and I took him with me. It was the coward in me more than anything else. I figured if he was with me when they found out I was getting six percent of their gross, nobody would be able to say or do anything much. Yes, I shamelessly used an eleven-year-old boy as a shield.

Meeting the headlining act sent Monty over the moon, and for the rest of the night, he glowed. Every time he talked about them, he called the members by their first names. Audra helped me sell Kiss Me Goodnight shirts in the lobby, and we ran out, which was a bonus because I think Daisy despaired of ever getting rid of that inventory. We had lots of questions about where to buy the music, and I handed out little cards with the band's web address printed on them. I'd made them on my computer and printed them on the last of my résumé paper. Now we needed to get some tracks loaded up for sale.

Dylan, Levi, Gavin, and Daisy had too little notice to be nervous before the show, so they had a lot of energy afterward. Daisy spent a lot of time hugging people. She became weepy and told everyone she loved them. Levi and Gavin rocked out to the headlining band and drank half the contents of the bar. Dylan found a quiet alcove in the lobby and herded me into it. He stood close, his chest inches from mine, dominating my personal space. Strangely, his proximity made the urge to wash my hands vanish.

"Have I thanked you for this yet?"

He had. Repeatedly. They all had. I nodded. More thanks wasn't necessary, but I didn't want to break the moment.

"It makes my head spin, how much you believe in my band." He caressed my cheek with the pad of his thumb.

I could feel the magnetism of his fingertips hovering a millimeter away from my skin. I think I started trembling. I wanted very badly for him to kiss me, but I was afraid if he did, he would only be doing it out of gratitude. I don't want his gratitude; I want him.

"I have a confession to make. I lied to get you this job."

He jerked back as if I'd slapped him, and his lips set in a firm line. "Lied?"

The urge to wash my hands returned. I wrung them together, but Dylan wasn't going to let me stall. He wrapped his hands around my wrists, iron bands keeping me from this soothing motion. I tried to pull away, but he only tightened his grip.

"Out with it, Lacey."

I took a deep breath. "They wouldn't negotiate with me until I told them I was your manager. I thought if I waited for one of you guys to make it downtown, it would be too late. The payment they're going to issue for tonight's performance will go to me. I'm supposed to take six percent and then pass the rest on to you. I won't take anything, of course. I'm sorry."

He stared at me. Seconds ticked by. Then he shook his head, never removing his distinctive teal gaze from mine. "You will take six percent. You earned it. Without you, we wouldn't be here. We wouldn't have just performed in front of thousands of people. Before this, we were lucky to get three hundred in the audience."

"Perhaps you should talk with the others first." I hung my head, the weight of my shame hurting all the way down my spine. Lying doesn't usually sit so heavily on me. Was I finally experiencing the cumulative effects of years of deceit?

"Hey," he said, and I looked up to once again drown in his eyes. "I know what the others will say. Trust me on this. We're all very much aware of how much you've contributed to this band."

I wasn't sure I would take the six percent, but we needed to stop arguing about it. I gave him a brief nod. My attention flickered between his deep eyes and his soft, kissable lips. *Please kiss me.*

His hands still encircled my wrists. He brought them up between us. "Lacey, I'm concerned about these. You've been washing them more and more. I can't be with you all the time. Are you using those gloves I sent you?"

I jerked back and tried to wrestle my hands from his hold. This was not the romantic scenario I'd envisioned. I'd wanted kissing and perhaps some inappropriate public groping, but that wasn't what Dylan had in mind.

I began to realize my compulsion was the major thing Dylan saw when he looked at me. I don't want to be his patient. I don't want him to spend our time together — or apart — analyzing all the things that are wrong with me.

Pain thumped hard in my chest as I realized this was never going to happen. Dylan doesn't dream about me the way I dream about him. He doesn't lie awake at night thinking of the way I smell or the way I felt in his arms when he kissed me. He doesn't long to snuggle on the sofa with me. I'm not even sure he remembers the implied significance of taking me out to watch the stars.

"Lacey." He held my wrists a little tighter, attempting to gain the upper hand in the struggle each of us tried simultaneously to win and to hide from anyone passing by.

"Let go of me," I growled, and he loosened his grip. I slid my hands free. They shook with fury. I'm not sure if I'm more pissed at him for only seeing my OCD or at myself for the five months I've spent pining for a man who isn't emotionally available.

He put one palm against the wall, blocking my easiest escape. "I worry about you."

I glared and didn't bother to temper my rage. "Then stop. I don't need another father, and I sure as hell don't need another shrink to tell me what's wrong with me. I am perfectly aware of my issues and how to deal with them." I paused, swallowing the lump in my throat and taking a ragged breath.

He reached for me. His hand hovered inches from my cheek, poised to deliver a soothing caress, but I flinched as if it were an incoming blow. I didn't want to be placated. If I've learned one thing over the years, it's to let my anger out when it grips me. If I subvert my feelings, my OCD only gets worse. I slapped his hand away.

He widened his eyes, and his mouth opened at my raw display. "Lacey, please don't be upset."

Upset? He hadn't seen nothing yet. "I didn't come here tonight for a lecture."

"Well, it's high time you got one." He set his jaw hard, the muscles there flexing as he ground his teeth. "Everybody thinks you're this quirky mess of a woman. They see that you're beautiful and charming, but equally fucked up. You aren't hiding anything, and you aren't fooling anybody."

That felt like a slap across the face. My expression must have shown it because Dylan flinched. He tried to pull me into his arms.

I brought my knee up sharply. I wasn't aiming for his manly parts, but he blocked anyway. Reflex, I suppose. I nailed him in the thigh, hard.

"Dammit, Lacey! I'm just trying to help you."

"Newsflash: I don't want your help." I pushed him back a step, opening up my path to freedom. I wanted his tenderness and affection. I wanted his kisses and his hands roaming my body. I didn't want another caretaker.

He looked at me, and desperation flashed across his face. "I care about you. A lot."

Yes, and he liked me too. I recognized the distinction between what he'd said and how I'd interpreted it.

I shook my head. "That doesn't make you my keeper."

He clenched his fists, and the teal in his eyes darkened ferociously. "You obstinate, inflexible woman. You're incapable of beating this alone. You need a keeper."

I itched to slap him. I am not incapable of beating this. I've made wonderful progress — recently too. Only I can't bring myself to tell him my story. But if I did, he'd certainly agree that I've come a long, long way back from the edge of sanity. He might then ease away slowly and avoid my phone calls, but he'd have to agree that my mental health has vastly improved.

Of course, even if I told my sad tale, I could never reveal all the details. Images of my baby brother assaulted my brain, his blood dripping through the slashes in his crib mattress and splattering on my hands as I hid beneath.

I felt the old fear seize me, and my tongue became paralyzed once again. I held fast to my anger at Dylan to keep from slipping back to the time when I couldn't talk, couldn't eat, couldn't move.

Breathe.

Just breathe.

It worked. I trembled, but I had myself back under control. Washing my hands was the least of my problems. Lying didn't even rate that high on the scale.

I slapped his chest with my open palm. "Fuck off, Dylan."

Then I stormed away. I had my wits about me, and I headed back into the main event area. I needed to get my jacket and keys, and the back door was closer to where I'd parked.

I muttered under my breath all the way to my car. People stared and moved out of my way. I probably looked crazy, but what the hell? I am crazy.

Chapter Ten

You might be thinking I went off the deep end. I didn't. Instead, I saw my life with blinding clarity: I'd been following Dylan around like a love-struck fan with a backstage pass, letting him reel me in and throw me back out whenever he wanted. I let him use me—differently from the way all my married exes had used me, but he'd used me just the same.

I went home, driving the speed limit the entire way. That envelope still lay on my table/desk, unopened and buried under a half-pound of paperwork. When I got home, I yanked it free, opened it, took a picture, and texted it to the number Thomas had given me.

I'm not your sister.

I was tempted, but I left off an invitation to fuck. The old Lacey couldn't have resisted the appeal of starting something she could lie her way out of. But now I'm the new Lacey. For the first time in my life, I don't want to lie. The idea turns my stomach. The excitement and peace I once found in the act are gone.

I wasn't expecting a response. It was after midnight on a Friday night more than two weeks after I was supposed to have contacted him. But my phone dinged immediately, startling me as I went to the bathroom to brush my teeth.

What are you doing tomorrow?

More than a little stunned, I stared at the message until my fingers remembered how to type. *Are you in town?*

I could be.

What did I have to lose? *I have no plans.*

Now you do.

I wasn't sure how to feel about not being asked. Well, I guess he technically did ask. *What plans do I have?*

Be at Detroit Metro at 2 pm. Bring a pretty evening dress and an overnight bag.

That made me leery. *Why?*

Bring ID and if you have them, take the nail clippers out of your purse.

I'm not getting on a plane without knowing where I'm going.

I wasn't sure I wanted to get on a plane at all, though Thomas's invitation intrigued me. The idea that our first date would involve a plane ride was surreal. I was apprehensive, but that wouldn't stop me from doing something rash. It never had before.

When my phone dinged again, the message was from Dylan. *Where are you?*

Washing my hands.

Ha ha. Seriously. I thought you went back in to watch the rest of the show.

Looks like he already checked the restrooms. Thomas's reply interrupted.

New York. Have you been? I want to take you to dinner at one of my favorite restaurants. I've booked a two-room suite for us overnight. We'll fly back Sunday at 10 am. Your ticket will be waiting.

That sounded very romantic. And forward. Thomas is the opposite of Dylan. My love life has been treading water for so long, this sudden forward progress threw me off. Does Thomas suffer from the same impetuousness that marks my personality? The idea merits further study.

Don't be angry. I'm not wrong.

I frowned at Dylan's reply. *You're not right, either.*

It's not a weakness to need somebody.

Son of a bitch. He truly does not understand me. All the time we've spent together, and he's missed what's right in front of his face.

Washing my hands means I'm coping, that I don't need anyone to watch out for me. He's probably a crappy therapist.

Thomas sent a follow up. *Lacey? We can do something in your area if you prefer.*

I didn't prefer. I wanted to get far, far away from Dylan. *New York sounds wonderful. I've never been, so you can be my tour guide.*

I added a smiley face and told him I was going to get some sleep.

I didn't reply to Dylan.

I slept solidly. Maybe the excitement of having broken things off with Dylan—though nothing had ever quite started—and my impending trip to New York combined with my extraordinary day to exhaust me.

I haven't seen Thomas in over a month. We have nothing between us but a dramatic lie, a dizzying kiss, and a DNA test. Now we have this weird trip thing. I have some questions about that.

The next day, he met me at the airport. I arrived in the main terminal to find him propped casually against a column. He wore a dark suit that highlighted his light brown hair. As I came closer, I noticed that his olive green tie made his eyes lean more toward green than brown. It was still a muddy color, but I found I liked that after staring so often at Dylan's unusual teal.

I took a moment to soak up his masculine attractiveness. He let me. Maybe he was taking a moment to soak up my beauty. I had taken a lot of time with my appearance today, and it was good to be appreciated.

At last he smiled and held out his hands to me. "Lacey. You're stunning, as always."

I slipped my hands into his. He lifted each to his lips and kissed it. Then he pulled me closer and lightly kissed my cheek. Our bodies didn't touch, but I felt his nearness, and his scent—sandalwood and mint—flooded my senses.

"I was starting to think you weren't going to call."

I blushed a little. "I wasn't sure if I should. I wasn't exactly nice to you."

He smiled. "You weren't mean. You panicked. I admire your courage."

Courage. Except for my parents, nobody had ever indicated I had any. I liked Thomas even more. Somehow he could see inside me.

"Thanks." I wanted to compliment him back, tell him I admired something about him, but I couldn't. I'd identified things about him I liked, but I hadn't idealized anything about him. "So, where are you taking me?"

His grin turned cocky, which emphasized his goatee in a very sexy way. "Dinner and a show." He held his hands out for my bag. "Our plane will be boarding soon. Let's get you checked in."

"Hold on," I said, my better sense finally making an appearance. "Thomas, this is all a little weird. You had a hotel already booked?" Was I a replacement date?

He laughed, but it was the ironic kind. "My buddy told me any woman worth my time would question the convenience of having a hotel, dinner reservations, and tickets to a Broadway show in hand the moment she sent me a text. I was wondering when you'd ask."

Holy shit. Apparently, I should've asked last night. I wonder if he'd doubted my sanity. Being tired, distraught, and furious worked as a convenient excuse, though now I wondered what the hell I'd been thinking. "I have asked, and I'm waiting on your answer."

"Well, the simple answer is: I didn't. The tickets and hotel room belonged to my mom, as did the dinner reservation, though that was always under my name. I had dinner with my mom last night. She told me she's divorcing my stepfather. She kicked him out yesterday, and she has no interest in seeing the show. She offered the tickets to me. I wasn't going to take them, but when I got your text, I figured it was fate."

I felt bad for his mother.

He stroked his goatee with a charming boyishness. "It's not the romantic impression I wanted to give, but it's the truth. And I did jump the gun a bit with my invitation. I called her to see if she'd given them away, and she didn't return my call until this morning. I did have a contingency plan, but it wasn't nearly as cool. First dates should be memorable, Lacey. I'm aiming to sweep you off your feet."

I stood silently for a moment while his story penetrated my brain. Usually silence weighs heavy on liars. Trust me on that. Unless they're fully committed to the lie, they get fidgety and try to amend their tale. Thomas didn't.

"Is your mother okay?"

He tilted his head, a brief frown on his face. Then he realized what I was asking. "Oh, yeah. This is her seventh divorce. They were together for about a year. She had a prenup, so she was protected."

Several hours and a plane ride later, we stood outside a restaurant set in an older building. It had white stone and fancy topiaries by the entrance. Thomas had rented a limousine, which picked us up from the airport and took us to the hotel. I'd changed into my dress, which from the way Thomas's jaw dropped, he admired. The bodice looked like someone had layered me in wide, white ribbons of satin. The skirt fell out from there, coming to the middle of my calves. It looked like a mess on the hanger, but it transformed into something special once I put it on. I could say it transformed me, but I'm already special.☺

I took my turn admiring the way he looked in a tuxedo. Yep, there'd been a lot of admiring going on. Then the driver transported us to this fancy place. Large letters above the door proclaimed "Daniel" in elegant script. In my entire life, I had never been anywhere this nice.

A doorman ushered us in, and the foyer screamed with class. From the large swirls on the carpet to the crystal chandeliers in the dining room, it looked like it was straight from a forties black-and-white film. I felt a little like Audrey Hepburn.

My dress fit in with the atmosphere, though I didn't have expensive jewelry or a pedigree to show off. I sort of felt like it was required at this place.

Thomas, it seemed, did. The maître d', a silver-haired man as elegant as his surroundings, smiled and nodded. "Mr. Pritchett. Welcome to Daniel. How was your flight?"

Thomas returned the man's greeting. "It was great. I had company this time. Ian Wexler, this is Lacey Hallem."

Ian turned his warm smile on me. "Ms. Hallem." He held out his hand. I gave him mine, and he bowed over it. Thank goodness he didn't kiss it. I don't have a thing about being touched, but I still don't like strangers getting familiar with me. Manners and chivalry be damned. Being a woman doesn't mean I give automatic consent to being pawed.

"Your table is ready. This is Julie." A petite brunette appeared at his side. Her serving uniform consisted of freshly pressed black slacks and a feminine, white button-down shirt. He put his hand on her shoulder. "She will show you to your seats."

She welcomed us with a pretty smile. "Mr. Pritchett, Ms. Hallem, please follow me."

As we entered the main dining room, I was blown away by the poshness of it all. More chandeliers hung from the ceiling, though the lighting was subdued. Everyone was dressed to the nines, and though I'd spent good money, my entire outfit probably cost as much as the toe of one shoe in this place.

Julie assured us she'd be back in a moment with the sommelier. I stared at her retreating back for a moment before I turned to Thomas.

"So…this is your favorite restaurant?"

He grinned. "One of them. I'm also trying really hard to impress you."

I was impressed, but not by the restaurant. I was impressed that he thought enough of me to believe that going all out was the only thing that would work. He'd even had a backup plan. I returned his grin. "Roses would have done the trick."

He waved his hand at me. "Too mundane. I'm sure you've had roses from dozens of men."

I have received flowers from several of the people I've dated, but most of my bouquets have come from one source. "My parents send me roses every Valentine's Day."

"See? It's no longer a romantic gesture."

Now that I thought about it, I guess I agreed. Even when my exes had come bearing flowers, I hadn't been dazzled—mostly because the flowers had come with an apology of some sort: *Sorry I canceled our date to spend the night with my wife. Sorry I didn't show up for lunch.*

My grin turned to a genuine smile. I'm finally with a man who isn't otherwise involved. Even Dylan still belongs to his deceased wife. I really need to stop thinking of him. Thomas dropped everything to spend the weekend with me. I never dreamed a man would do that, not for me.

"This is really going to make the second date difficult." I gave him the full flirt—hair twirling and everything.

"How do you figure?"

"How do you top this?"

Julie returned with the sommelier, and we paused our bantering to choose a wine. I didn't know much about that. Though I've been on several wine tours, I've only learned that too much wine gives me a headache. Thomas chose for us.

I sipped his selection. It was fruity and a little dry.

He leaned closer. Our table had plush benches arranged in an L-shape. A throw pillow separated us, but we were still very close together. "I get the sense you're the kind of woman who isn't truly impressed by anything but the quality of a man's character."

Considering I'd screamed an accusation at him and later confessed to being a compulsive liar, I'm not sure where he was getting his information. I had to challenge his flattering assumption. "Then why all the bells and whistles on the first date?"

He considered this for a few heartbeats, studying my face as he did so. "You met me under peculiar circumstances. I want you to know who I really am."

I looked around at the fine dining room. Our table had higher quality linens and flatware than I ever hoped to own. If this was him, what did he think he had in common with me? I confess to being more than a little baffled.

"You're a fancy restaurant with high-end fixtures?" That came out cold, and I hadn't intended to be bitchy. Luckily, Thomas didn't seem affected.

"Sometimes." He looked at me, his gaze searching my eyes. "Maybe more often than I'd like."

I heard the longing in his voice, a desire for more than material goods, and I responded. "I'm not from around here." I'm solidly middle-class. Or I aspire to be.

A slow grin spread across his face, lifting one side of his mouth and then the other. The net effect was a charmingly crooked smile. "That's why I like you."

"I probably won't fit in with your friends and family." Maybe he just wants me for sex? I could be making a huge leap here.

His grin didn't waver. "You don't know that. I think they'll love you."

I looked down at my place setting. "I don't even know which forks or spoons to use for what." Though at least I know I'm supposed to use them for different things. One is for salad, another for tea or coffee. If they were in my kitchen, they'd all be jumbled in a drawer. And I'd have six or twelve of each.

He put his hand on the table, palm up, silently asking for mine. I studied his fingers. They were long and trim, shaped quite well. I'm not sure why I notice these kinds of details. Before too long, I gave him my hand. I thought he would make some kind of move, but he only held it in his.

"Lacey, no more putting yourself down. I know who you are. You blew me away the first moment I saw you, and every minute I spend with you only makes me like you more. I didn't ask you out because I thought you could differentiate silverware. I can teach you those things, if you want. I asked you out because I like you."

That made me feel a little better, but I couldn't stop wondering what he'd tell people when they asked how we met.

The rest of the night flew by. I ate turbot, which was a word I'd only heard on television. It turned out to be fish, and the chef at Daniel was incredible, so it was tasty fish. I was able to cut it into eighteen pieces. After dinner, Thomas took me to see a play I'd heard about but never thought I'd actually see. He held my hand through most of the performance. All in all, it was a wonderful evening.

Standing at the door of the suite, waiting for him to unlock it with the keycard, I decided tonight would have an exceptionally good ending. It had been two years since the last time I was with a man. My imaginary adventures with Davey, Simon, and Jared were wonderful, but nothing could substitute for the feel of skin sliding against mine and the scent of a real, live man.

"I had a great time with you tonight." Thomas held the door open for me.

For a second, I thought he might not follow me inside, but it was a two-bedroom suite, and we'd already claimed our separate spaces. I debated whether I wanted to sleep with him in my room or his. Did I want to stick around afterward, or did I want to slink away to sleep alone?

These are questions I rarely consider. My other boyfriends hadn't been able to stay with me most nights. Would waking up naked next to a man who'd rocked my world make me fall in love? I truly didn't know.

I offered a cheeky grin as I waited for him inside the living room/kitchenette area of the suite. "Yeah. It wasn't bad."

He secured the locks and caught my flirtatious tone. "Not bad?"

I slid my arms around his neck. "I can't give it a firm score without a goodnight kiss."

He threw his keycard on a nearby table and parked his hands on my waist. "I've been looking forward to this since the last time you kissed me."

"I'll try not to make this one so sisterly."

His lips were hot and firm. We massaged and tasted, dancing around each other's tongues. He was a feast for my senses—his smell, the tickle of his goatee against my face, and the feel of his strong body pressed against mine. I wound my fingers through his hair, searching for a handhold that wasn't there.

I must have made a desperate mewling sound, and I'll attribute the manly groan to him. He picked me up, crushing me to him, and carried me to the sofa. I wasn't the most compliant load. I bit his lower lip and tried to wrap my body around his. There was no sense preserving modesty when we'd both soon be naked.

He tried to put me down gently, but I tugged at him too hard, and he tumbled down on top of me.

I held him close as he tried to adjust his weight so he wasn't squashing me. I wanted him to squash me—I wanted confirmation that he could engulf me. I let him rearrange our limbs before I demanded his lips back.

I snatched and ripped at his clothes until his jacket was gone and his tie was loose. I caressed his thighs and hips with my legs as best I could. The back of the sofa and the tightness of my dress inhibited my range. He explored my neck and the exposed parts of my upper chest with his lips. I loved the feel of his facial hair scratching and tickling my skin. I wanted to know if it would feel as good between my thighs. Looking around with bleary eyes, I decided we needed more space.

Frantically, I ran my hands over his shirt, soaking up the heat that penetrated the fabric. "Thomas, let's go to the bedroom." I didn't specify which one. At this point, I didn't care. "I think we need more room."

He stopped what he was doing and stared down at me. Taking a deep, ragged breath, he propped his weight up on one hand. "No."

"No?" Yep, I echoed him like a parrot. No man had ever turned me down before.

He knelt and pulled me up with him. Now I sat next to him on the sofa instead of being under him in bed. He threaded his fingers through mine, just as he had at the play. "No. You're sexy and charming, and I click with you in a way I haven't clicked with anybody in a long time. I don't want to rush this. I want to savor it."

I wanted to savor it too. In the bedroom. All night long, if he was up for it.

"I also don't want you to think I went through all this trouble just to get you into bed. I did it because this was the first date I fantasized about having with you, something amazing that would make you want to spend more time with me."

If I offered to be his dream come true in more ways than that, would it sound too much like a porno line? I thought about arguing for exactly one half of a second. Then I snuggled my head onto his shoulder. I could have seduced him, but I guess the ease with which I gave in showed I wasn't as gung-ho to sleep with him as I'd thought.

Still, I had to push the issue. "You didn't fantasize about sleeping with me?"

He shook his head. "I've planned it, but I haven't fantasized about it."

I truly did not see the distinction. Maybe he thought the latter was a girl thing. "You planned it? For when?"

"I live in Connecticut, and you're in Michigan. We're not exclusive; we're just getting to know one another. I don't know your favorite color or what kind of music you like. I was thinking the fifth date."

Assigning a number was a mistake. My OCD kicked in, and I corrected him. "The sixth." It was not a negotiation.

"Okay," he said. "I'll seduce you on the sixth date. Things between us will be serious by then."

I hope I can hold out that long.

Chapter Eleven

Thomas didn't fly back with me. We went to the airport together and boarded separate planes. After we decided not to have sex until the sixth date, we'd spent another hour engaging in conversation punctuated by bouts of heavy petting. Not only was it more action than I'd seen in the past six months, it was damn good action. I'd truly believed my crush on Dylan—and my obsession with the breadcrumbs of affection he dropped every now and again—had ruined me for other men. But being with Thomas proved I was alive and vital, and an attractive man wanted to be with me. It shouldn't have mattered, but it did. My vibrator boyfriends could only keep me occupied for so long.

Exhaustion had eventually driven us to our separate bedrooms, and we'd slept until the front desk called to wake us at the appointed time. Thomas had thought of everything.

Back home, I met Luma for an early dinner. I'd skipped lunch, so I was famished. Between bites, I told her about my extraordinary date. It was no surprise she didn't buy it.

"So you've suddenly decided to give up on Dylan, and this new guy flies you to New York for his version of dinner and a show?"

She regarded me with open and obvious disbelief. The asparagus tip she'd speared slid from her fork and dropped onto her plate. She didn't go after it.

"Yes."

"Are you lying?"

I shook my head. "I know. It sounds like something fantastic I'd make up, but I didn't. It happened."

"Is he married?"

Again I gave her a negative answer. "And he knows I lie."

She stared at me with a calculating look. I've never told any man I dated about that part of my compulsion, and lies have derailed all of my relationships.

"Did you sleep with him?"

Not for lack of trying. "No. We're waiting until the sixth date."

"Wait. He spent thousands of dollars on a date with you, and he didn't try to score?" Her dark eyes widened.

"I know, right? I tried, though. He's the one who wants to wait. He said we have time."

She dropped her fork dramatically. It hit the table, but it didn't clatter like she probably meant for it to. "He's gay."

Hard evidence of his straightness had made itself known several times while we kissed and rubbed our bodies together. "No. I think he's a bit of an idealist. After everything he knows about me, he still has me up on a pedestal. I'm not sure I should respect him for that."

She picked up her fork, wiped it on her napkin, and took a bite of her food. "You think he's missing a few brain cells because he thinks highly of you? I think you're selling yourself short, yet again."

As I've said before, I don't have a great track record. I don't look at myself and see qualities that would attract other people. "Maybe I just really wanted to have sex. He's a very good kisser, and he puts his hands in the right spots."

She giggled. "If he'd put his hands in the right spots, you wouldn't be complaining about not getting any last night."

"True, but that's not what I meant. I'm trying to say he's good with his hands. Perfect placement, perfect pressure. You know when you're making out with some guy, and he puts his hand in an awkward place?"

Luma wrinkled her nose. I could tell she was trying to not laugh. She lost that battle and decided to mock me. "Like when he's reaching for your hoo-ha, and he finds your nuh-uh?"

"No, but that's a mood-killer too. I mean like when he's holding you up, and he's only supporting half your back. You have to work to stay level or take a nasty fall. Or when one finger presses too hard into your lower back or your thigh. That one off thing is all you can think about, and it ruins everything."

She stopped laughing long enough to commiserate. "Yeah. I had a date like that last weekend. I had to make him stop touching me, and even then he kept trying to hold my hand. I was so glad I'd driven my car over. Nothing makes a bad date worse than needing a ride home after you tell a guy he sucks ass."

Silence fell as we digested a bit. I knew Luma still didn't believe me.

"Luma? I swear this happened."

She shrugged. "You've been mooning over Dylan for months, and then you come up with this fairy-tale story? It's too convenient, Lace. Your lies tend to be outlandish and convenient. This hits both marks, dead center."

I had the ticket stub from the show in my purse. I dug it out and shoved it across the table at her. "Maybe I deserve to have the fairy tale. Maybe I finally deserve to be with a guy who doesn't have another woman in the back of his mind. Thomas cares about me."

He truly does. I have no idea why, but he does.

Luma opened her mouth, but I cut her off. "Except for pretending to be the band manager for Kiss Me Goodnight, which I don't really count, I haven't lied in months — not to you or anybody else — and it feels like a new normal. If I continue to wait for Dylan to see me as a woman instead of a mentally unstable friend, I'll die alone. I'm moving on. I need someone like Thomas in my life, someone who knows the real me and likes me anyway."

I think that's the first time I've ever snapped at Luma. Tears tracked down my cheeks, and I rubbed angrily at them. The wetness on my fingers triggered a deep longing to wash my hands. I rose to my feet.

Luma grabbed my arm. "I'm sorry. I'm happy for you, Lacey. You're right; you deserve the fairy tale. I'm just...I...I thought you were head over feet for Dylan."

"Dylan had his chance. I've moved on."

That was a lie unlike any I've ever told. It wasn't exactly an untruth, just an oversimplification. I haven't moved on, but I've made up my mind to do so. I think Luma recognized my resolve. She released my arm. I went to the bathroom and washed my hands six times.

Jane called later that evening to offer her support. Luma and I had left things on a positive note, but the fact that she spilled her guts to Jane meant she felt guilty for doubting me. Or that she still doubted me and wanted to see if Jane would get the same story. I'm a consummate liar, but I can't keep an outlandish story straight for longer than it takes to tell. These details were not hard to recall.

Within ten minutes of hanging up with Jane, my mother called.

"John is home from the hospital."

I didn't know John had been in the hospital. "What happened?"

"He had some chest pain and shortness of breath."

I knew the indicators for a heart attack. John's parents had both died from heart-related problems, and his brother had heart-valve surgery last year. "Mom! Why didn't you call me?"

"Well, it was the middle of the night, and we didn't know what was wrong. I didn't want to worry you."

I closed my eyes and counted to eighteen. She didn't sound too concerned, and my mother wasn't the kind of woman who would downplay a significant event. Was there a point to arguing with her after the fact?

"What did the doctors say?"

She sighed. "That he needs to take aspirin, which he hadn't been doing even though his regular doctor told him to do it months ago. We're going to see a nutritionist tomorrow, and we're going to start an exercise regimen. Apparently, walking Sadie around the yard until she does her business isn't enough."

I was the one who took Sadie out for her longer walks every few days, so I knew how little exercise John got. He was tall and thin, but not healthy. I swallowed hard. "Mom? He's taking this seriously, right?"

It would be just like him to blow it off. Bad things happened to other people, not John Zimmerman. As he liked to say, fate had brought me and my mother into his life, and he'd promised never to let go of us.

"Yes, sweetheart. We both are. We're going to get fit together. I boxed up my old cookbooks. They're in the basement, if you want them. I've ordered a bunch of newer ones with healthy meals."

My mother loved dessert. She made the best cakes and pies. For her to put away her beloved recipes meant she was more afraid than she was letting on. Knowing that, I couldn't hold on to my anger. As always, she was protecting me, trying to avoid triggering my lying and hand washing. Hot tears pricked at my eyes. "I have tomorrow off. Can I come over for a visit?"

"Of course. You're always welcome at home. Why don't you come for lunch?"

"I'll be there."

John was in good spirits when he answered the door the next morning. He hugged me for an extra long time, reassuring me with his physical presence. He felt solid and strong, the same way he always has, and I found that comforting.

"Genevieve made some kind of slaw with carrots and parsnips. It's good, but it's not carrot cake. I think that's going to be the hardest part—giving up your mother's treats."

I kept my arm around his waist as we walked to the kitchen. "I don't think you have to give them up. I think you just need smaller portions and maybe cut back to once a week."

He leaned down and kissed the top of my head. "I like the way you think. If we work together, we can convince your mother to come over to our side."

If my mother had drawn a hard line in the sand, I wasn't about to cross it. She rarely took a firm stand, but when she did, woe to anyone who didn't bow to her edict. So, I did what any sensible person would do: abandoned ship. "Sorry, John. If Mom says no, you know what that means."

He snorted. "You've always been such a good girl."

"Yes, she has." My mom set a dish towel on the counter and hugged me tighter than John had. I felt the fear she was trying to hide. New lines had sprouted around her mouth, and dark circles had taken up residence under her eyes.

"Mom, you have to promise you'll call me immediately if anything happens again, no matter how small."

She gave a tiny nod, the only outward indication that she knew she was in over her head. Then she patted my shoulder dismissively. "Lacey, hon, help John set the table."

Ten minutes later, I had revised my view of healthy food. With my mother cooking, dishes that should be disgusting were actually tasty. I would never have thought eggplant steaks could be good, yet I asked for seconds.

John tried to steer the conversation away from his health. He succeeded by asking about my weekend. Like Luma, after I told him where I'd been and with whom, he asked the golden question: "Are you lying?"

I was ready for this one. I shook my head and showed him my ticket stub. Where Luma needed convincing, my mom started crying. I think some of it was the stress of her weekend.

"Honey, this is so wonderful. You've come so far. I'm so proud of you." She got up and snagged a tissue from the next room. "Though I'm not sure how I feel about you dating someone who flies you to another state for the night."

I assured her Thomas had good intentions. "He's a great guy, Mom. If he wasn't, I wouldn't have gone anywhere with him. And he's nice. I think you'll like him."

My mom sat back down at the table. "Well, then, I'm looking forward to meeting him."

John, sitting next to her, held her hand in his. "I'm sorry things haven't worked out with Dylan. I know you liked him, but five months without a lie? That's amazing. You've never gone more than a week before. This is a breakthrough. How does it feel?"

It felt wonderful. Truly wonderful. Except now I had to come clean about the white lie I'd told. I cleared my throat. "I did tell one lie this weekend. I told the people at The Fillmore I was the manager of Dylan's band so I could negotiate with them. I told Dylan, and he wasn't upset, but he also doesn't know I lie. Thomas does, though."

John studied me carefully, and I knew he'd shifted to view me through his therapist's lens. I didn't mind, because he'd actually been my therapist. I trusted him implicitly.

"Lacey, the fact that you're telling white lies is progress. You never went in for the little things. I'm not saying lying is right, but what you've done is actually quite healthy."

That made me feel even better.

I wanted to put it off, but I had to drop by Daisy's house the next day. The Fillmore had paid me for the band's performance, and I needed to pass that money on. I texted Daisy to see if she was going to be home. On a Tuesday afternoon, I expected everybody else to be at work. I was wrong.

Levi answered the door. He pulled me into the house, lifted me up, and swung me in a circle. "You know, the first time I met you, I remember thinking you were one ballsy chick. I was right."

I couldn't recall the last time someone had been so effervescent in their greeting. I laughed, trying to sound happy instead of nervous. The living room was full of people. Levi set me down, and Daisy took up where he left off. Thankfully, she only hugged me. Then Gavin took his turn. He set me in front of Dylan and shoved my shoulder, urging me closer to Dylan. I resisted.

I didn't know if he was angry with me for telling him to fuck off or if I was still upset with him for treating me like a client.

He offered a tight smile. "Thanks, Lacey. Because of you, we've had two radio stations ask for a single."

"That's wonderful." I was genuinely delighted for him. For them all. I directed my congratulations at the group. "You guys deserve it. Hopefully you can get some air time in a major market like Los Angeles or New York."

The tension between Dylan and me was thick, and the rest of the band would've had to be incredibly clueless not to pick up on it. They weren't. The cheerful sounds in the room quieted.

I extracted my wallet from my purse. "I wasn't sure how you wanted it, so I brought one check. You guys probably want to put it aside for studio time or new equipment or something."

They had other jobs, and the paltry pay from their shows wasn't enough to use for income so they'd been putting that money into a pool to use for the band's expenses. On the plus side, they were now self-supporting. I'd never asked if they had any surplus. It wasn't my business.

Dylan looked at the amount. "You didn't take your six percent."

I shrugged. I didn't need the money. "I didn't do anything much."

He glowered at me, and I took a step back, edging toward the door. I wasn't afraid, but I didn't have anything left for a fight. John might have looked fine, but I'd spent the night tossing and turning, waiting for the call that would confirm my worst fears.

Gavin put his hands on my shoulders and spun me to face him. The tension building between Dylan and me didn't fade, but it stopped growing. Gavin grinned. "Daisy said you'd refuse the money. That's okay. We have a better deal. We want to hire you to be our manager."

I studied his face, looking for signs he was fooling with me. Gavin had a great sense of humor, but sometimes he was the only one in on the joke.

Daisy spoke next. "You don't have to answer right now. You can take some time to think about it."

They were serious. "I don't know how to be a manager. You should get somebody with experience. Or at least somebody who has an idea of what they're doing." I scanned the crowd. They stood around me in a semicircle. From their expressions they seemed to disagree with me.

Levi gave voice to their opposition. "As I said, you've got balls. Brass ones. We want you."

"Courage," Dylan chimed in. "He means you have courage. You can tell Levi doesn't write our lyrics. He has a limited vocabulary."

Daisy took my hand. "Lacey, you got us a gig opening for Walk the Moon, and you weren't even trying. You can do anything."

I didn't have that kind of confidence in me. "It was dumb luck. I was in the right place at the right time. You don't want to entrust your future to me."

"Six months," Daisy said. "Let's try it for six months. At the end of that time, if either party wants to dissolve the contract for any reason, we can."

"Contract?" They wanted a legal relationship? That scared me more than anything. It put responsibilities on my shoulders I wasn't sure the skin of my hands could take.

Dylan handed me a green folder. "It's in there. You get twelve percent to start. We already signed it."

They weren't going to let me get away with a straight refusal. I clutched the folder to my chest, but I didn't look inside. "I'll think about it, but not right now. I have to meet a client, so I need to get going."

During the farewell process, I caught more than a few accusatory glares directed at Dylan. I wondered if he'd told them about our argument.

I made it two steps from my car before he came after me.

"Lacey, wait up a second."

Pausing on the strip of grass between the sidewalk and the street, I pivoted in time to see his magnificent figure jogging toward me. I would like to say I took this time to compare him unfavorably to Thomas, but I didn't. Dylan is hot; nobody else comes close.

I peered up at him with what I hoped was a neutral expression. He didn't need to know I would welcome him shoving me against my car to make out in public. Nope. Hell, I was better off not knowing that.

"I wanted to apologize for Friday night. I didn't mean to upset you. I care about you—"

"I know you care about me, Dylan." That's sort of the problem. If he cared a little less, he might feel free to make a move. Or not. With my luck, today is his wife's birthday. I had so many things I wanted to say to him, none of them appropriate. I settled for meeting him halfway. "I'm not mad at you anymore."

He grinned, and his eyes sparkled in the sunlight. A breeze played with a lock of hair on his forehead. I noticed these details, and wished I didn't.

"I knew giving you a few days to cool off was the right move. You're not the kind of person who holds a grudge for very long."

I sighed. I don't hold grudges because I usually don't care enough to stay angry. "John was in the hospital Sunday with signs of a heart attack. He didn't have one, but it was close."

He could assume I'd been at John's side through it all. If my mother had called, that would've been the case. Did this count as a lie? I honestly don't know.

"I'm sorry to hear that. He's okay now?"

I nodded. "They're changing their exercise and eating habits. John has a history of heart disease in his family, so we're taking it very seriously."

"Good." He hesitated, ruffling his hair with his hand. "If you need me, you can call. Anytime."

"Thanks." I turned, hitting the button to unlock my car. The conversation was made awkward by what wasn't being said. I knew he wanted to bring up my hand-washing, and I desperately didn't want to mention where I'd been or who I'd been with.

"Lacey?"

I didn't want to face him again, but I did.

"Think about it, okay? You'll make a great manager."

Chapter Twelve

Two nights later, on my way home from dinner with Mom and John, my cell rang. I turned down the radio and answered it.

"What are you doing this weekend?"

"Thomas. I was just thinking about you."

I swear I could hear him smile on the other end of the line. "I know. I'm psychic."

During my deliberations, I'd come to the conclusion that Thomas would be an objective sounding board for the idea of me managing Kiss Me Goodnight. Luma and Jane both thought I should jump at the opportunity, but I wanted an unbiased opinion. "I wanted to ask your advice on something."

"Really?" He sounded pleased.

"Yeah. Did you get those tracks I sent you?"

"The ones from your friends' band? Yep. They sound great."

"They want me to manage them." I explained about the six-month contract. He already knew about the opening gig I'd landed for them. I'd used the story to make him laugh on our date. The fact that my lying didn't put him off made me feel like I could take more emotional chances with him.

"What percentage did they offer? Or did they go for a straight salary?"

I gave him the details. He asked questions that had never occurred to me, confirming my decision to ask for his counsel. His business experience far exceeded mine.

"Fax me the contract. I'll take closer look and talk to a buddy who has some experience managing musical talent. Now, let's get back to the original reason I called. What are you doing this weekend?"

Other than checking on my mom and John, I didn't have plans. "I was hoping to see you."

"I'm in Chicago until Friday. Is there any chance I can convince you to meet me for dinner? We could make a weekend of it — see the aquarium, stuff like that. And it's close enough that I can get you home in under an hour if an emergency arises."

He was so thoughtful. I'd told him about John's health scare. He'd been there for his father, though they weren't as close as John and me, and he understood that I needed to be near.

By that evening, he'd emailed me his analysis. Not only did he enthusiastically encourage me to take on the contract when I met him that Friday in Chicago, but shortly thereafter his friend who managed talent contacted me and related lots of advice. Within a week of broaching the subject with Thomas, I had a list of contacts around the country and a name to drop.

With those tools and Kiss Me Goodnight's rave reviews from their one opening gig, it didn't take long to book them several weekend dates at smaller venues. The band thought I was the second coming.

"You're amazing," Daisy said the following week as she folded laundry on her kitchen table.

I'd stopped by to clear a Philadelphia date with her. The rest of the band was pretty mobile, but Daisy needed notice so she could make sure Audra was available to take care of Monty. The other shows I'd booked had been closer to home — journeys no farther than a three- or four-hour car ride.

"I can't believe you thought you'd make a crappy manager," she continued. "You've done more in two weeks than any of us have been able to do in six months."

I couldn't take credit for everything. Though I landed them that gig at The Fillmore, everything else had come from Thomas. I might have blushed under Daisy's praise. Receiving compliments has never been my strong suit.

"It wasn't all me. I mentioned what I'm doing to Thomas, and he knows someone who's been doing this for years. That's where I got the contact information, and the rest is all you guys. I send them a couple of your tracks, and they're foaming at the mouth to book you."

She stopped in the midst of folding a shirt. "Thomas?"

We'd been on two dates, and I'd only mentioned him to my parents, Luma, and Jane. I don't know if I purposely didn't mention him to the band or if he'd just never come up before. Maybe a little of both.

My blush deepened, heating my cheeks and chest. "He's…a friend." We weren't exclusive, but I didn't make out with my friends, so that lie didn't sit well with me. "We've gone out a couple of times."

She smacked my arm. The slap rang in the air. Startled, I jumped back and fell out of my chair. I hit the floor with a thud that rattled my backside.

Daisy rushed to help me. "I didn't hit you that hard."

My father broke my femur when I was eighteen months old. I don't have any memory of it, but I've always been a flincher. My mom blames my father. I don't know who's at fault; I just know I don't relish being hit. I don't think that's unusual.

I popped back into the chair as if I'd never left it. "I'm fine. Thanks." She looked at me funny, and I feared she'd ask a question I couldn't answer without lying. I barreled forward. "He's a great guy. He took me to Chicago last weekend and New York the weekend before. He lives in Connecticut."

Her suspicious, speculative expression turned tart, and she frowned. "What about you and Dylan?"

"There is no 'me and Dylan.' He's not over his wife."

She snorted and shook another piece of clothing free from the pile in her basket. "He's over Nadia. I think he was over her before she passed away."

The ring he'd worn around his neck at their first concert—though I hadn't seen him wear it since—testified to the opposite. "He told me he wasn't over her."

"He did not." Daisy's disapproving frown dared me to challenge her.

You know how I react to dares, right? "Yes, he did. He wore her ring to his first performance. When he took me to look at the stars, he said he wasn't ready to move on. He told me I was fucked up. Am I supposed to spend my life waiting for him? I'm not going to suddenly turn into a different person. I don't want to. I like myself just fine. Thomas knows a lot more about me than Dylan does, and he doesn't call me names or treat me like a kid who needs a babysitter. He likes me, Daisy. He likes *me*."

I didn't say the rest of what I was thinking. While I truly liked Thomas, I wanted Dylan with an urgency that left me fractured and breathless. On paper, Thomas was perfect. I desperately wanted to want him the most.

"That explains why you've been happier the past couple weeks. I thought maybe you and Dylan had finally gotten together."

Silently, I shook my head. If that had happened, I would've been ecstatic. Dylan and I had done the opposite of getting together; we'd cooled down completely.

When someone pounded on my door that evening, I expected my neighbor, Pauline. She's in her nineties and hard of hearing. The way she speaks to me and knocks on my door indicates that she assumes I also suffer from hearing loss.

She likes to bring me baked goods every now and again. I invite her in and make tea. We chat, and sometimes she forgets I'm not her great-grandchild and starts talking to me about her daughter, whom she refers to as "your grandmother." I never correct her. We aren't related, but I don't have a grandmother, and Pauline is a nice substitute.

I'd been stretching and thinking of Thomas. Some might call it an attempt at yoga (the stretching, not the thinking, though sometimes that's up for debate too), but I don't think I'm there yet. I'm not sure if I'll ever get there, but I look cute in the pants, and they're comfortable to boot. Stretching made me feel like I'd earned the right to wear them while vegging and scarfing popcorn, which was my real plan.

Thomas had sent me a dress that hugged my curves in sinful and suggestive ways. The note with it said he was looking forward to seeing me wear it. He'd sent matching shoes and a purse, but he wouldn't tell me where we were going. I predicted dinner, since the plane ticket put me in Boston at four on Friday.

At any rate, I did not expect to see Dylan, fist raised to thump on my door again, when I opened it. He must have caught the security door downstairs as someone was going out.

He wore jeans that were worn and faded, and he looked incredible. On top, he had the AFI *Black Sails* shirt he'd been wearing when we met. It did not suffer from coffee stains.

His chest heaved like he'd run a long way, and he gripped his car keys tightly. He stormed into my apartment and slammed the door shut.

"Who the hell is Thomas?"

I blinked at him as I pondered which side of the door I wanted him on before I locked it. How could someone look sexy and thunderous at the same time? I did not find his display of temper charming. When men yell at me, I tend to leave and not come back.

But I wasn't afraid of Dylan, so I voted to let him stay. I locked the door in case someone else who was pissed came a-knocking.

"Hello, Dylan. So nice to see you. I take it Daisy told you about Philly."

That deflated his black sails a little. "Yeah. That's awesome. Thanks." He shoved a hand in his pocket and lowered his volume. "That's not why I'm here."

I gestured toward the sofa. "Want to sit down, or would your point be better made standing and shouting?"

He paced three steps toward the far end of the room, bypassing the sofa. "Lacey, who is Thomas?"

Do I owe him an explanation? No, but it would be petty of me not to answer. "Thomas is a man I'm seeing. We've gone out a couple of times. He's the one who made it possible for me to book dates for your band."

He blinked at me, speechless.

"Daisy didn't tell you?"

He found his voice, but not his sense. "Are you sleeping with him to book dates for my band?"

I'm not sure what expression came to my face, but it must have communicated sufficient outrage. He backpedaled. "Lacey, that didn't come out right."

No, it didn't. I'm not sure there's any right way for that to come out. "I think you should go."

"No, wait." He captured my arms in his firm grasp. "I'm sorry. Daisy told me you had a boyfriend, and I freaked out."

I wanted to say something flip or cool, but I'm neither flip nor cool when I really need to be. "He's not my boyfriend."

Interest lit his eyes. He lifted his brows. "No?"

"No, but he has plans along those lines. He lives in another state. We're letting things unfold naturally. Long distance is hard enough without forcing the issue."

His eyes blazed. "I told you I like you."

"You can't call dibs on a woman and walk away. It doesn't work like that."

He kissed me, skipping the preamble and going straight for my lips. I let him. I wanted this so badly. Thoughts of everything but the way Dylan made me feel this very moment flew from my head. He released my arms and wrapped me in his embrace.

I clutched his shoulders and gave as good as I got. He tasted like cherry Lifesavers and smelled like heaven. This time, I didn't hold back. I slid one hand up the back of his neck and sank my fingers into his thick hair.

He broke the kiss, but he didn't stop. He nibbled at my lower lip and tangled a hand in my hair. With a slow tug, he urged my head back and gained access to my neck. Heat seared my skin as he tracked kisses along my throat. I moaned.

The few times he'd kissed me before, he'd stopped at moments like this. I didn't want that to happen again. If he stopped, I would incinerate from the latent power of unfulfilled longing. I shoved his shirt out of the way so I could explore his abs. They were rock hard. A sprinkling of hair marked the center and tickled against my palm.

I slid my hands lower, teasing at the waist of his jeans, and he growled. "Bedroom."

"Yes." I jumped up onto him, wrapping my legs around his mid-section.

He cupped my ass in his hands and held me against his body as he continued kissing me. It wasn't a smooth ride to my room. He stumbled several times, conveniently pinning me to the wall where he grinded against me, and then he crashed me into the closed bedroom door. I fumbled it open, and we fell through and onto the bed.

Dylan landed heavily on top of me. I looked up to find him grinning in triumph, and I knew he'd tripped on purpose. I didn't care. I finally had him where I wanted him. The grin on his lips faded, and his eyes turned somber. He didn't say anything, but when he kissed me, his thoroughness said it all.

He wanted me.

He drew his palm down the center of my chest, bypassing both breasts. He lifted my shirt and bared a few inches above my yoga pants. I writhed, seeking more of his caress and less clothing between us. Thank goodness for these pants. They allowed me to feel every brush and caress.

Breaking away suddenly, he scooted me until I was centered on the bed, and then he peppered kisses along my midsection. Slowly, he worked his way up, pushing my shirt out of the way as he went. I wanted to feel his hands and mouth on my breasts so badly they tingled.

I arched my body against his, seeking more friction between my legs. I wouldn't have minded a quick release of the tension that had built between us for months. We had time for a leisurely exploration afterward. I tore at his shirt, and he shifted around to help me remove it.

This wasn't the first time I'd seen him without a shirt—he'd stripped down in the band's dressing room, exchanging a sweat-soaked number for something fresh after a show—but this was the best one so far.

"Lovely. So beautiful." He unsnapped my bra, and as he lifted the cups away from my breasts, he whispered, "Nadia."

Throwing a glass of ice water on me would have been nicer. I smacked at his shoulder and shoved him. "Get off me."

He stopped and blinked up at me. "Huh?"

I used his momentary confusion to slide out from beneath him. "You called me Nadia." I turned my back and fixed my clothes. "Get out."

He sat up, parking his ass on his heels and his hands on his thighs. "I didn't mean to."

Neither had at least two of my married boyfriends. And because they'd "loved" me, I'd gone out of my way to be understanding. Forgiveness had been easy because I hadn't felt worthy of having a man to myself. Things were different now. I wanted more. I wanted it all. Fury wrapped around my heart. "Doesn't matter."

"It does matter, or else you wouldn't be throwing me out." He reached for me, but I backed away, shaking so hard my teeth chattered.

"You're not over her."

"I'm over her."

There was no point in arguing. I knew I was right. I closed my eyes, trying to stop the gathering storm, but tears spilled down my cheeks. The angrier I became, the harder it was to keep from crying.

"Lacey." He reached for me again, this time getting up and coming toward me.

He may as well have tried to hit me. I backed away, not stopping until I bumped against the window. "No. Don't touch me. I'm not doing this. I promised myself I was worth more than being a secondhand lover."

He wrinkled his brows and spread his palms. "What's that supposed to mean?"

"It means I'm not going to be the replacement woman. I deserve more from a man than that. I deserve a man who likes me for me, who wants to be with me and nobody else."

"I agree." He clamped his hands on my shoulders. "I want to be with you and nobody else. That's why I'm here — to prove that to you."

He'd done quite the opposite. I shook my head.

"Lacey, you're being unreasonable."

Item number one on the list of things not to say to a woman who is hurt and angry, and he'd said it. My temper erupted through my damn tears. "Unreasonable? Is it unreasonable to expect you to get my name right? For you to remember who you're fucking?"

I tore from his hold, scooped up his shirt, and threw it at him.

"I have rotten taste in men. The first man I dated was married. So was the second. It started an inescapable and vicious cycle of settling for men whose hearts belonged to other women." I realized I was shouting and lowered my voice to just above a wobbly snarl. "Two years ago, after I broke it off with the last one, I promised myself I would never do it again. I'm worth somebody's whole heart. I want it all, or I want nothing. I haven't really dated anyone in two years because every single time I find one I like, he's married. I thought you were married the first moment I saw you."

Dylan tugged his shirt over his head and tried to pull me into his arms.

I scrambled away, holding up my hand as a warning between us. "Thomas isn't married. He has no ex-wife or dead wife who already owns his heart. He likes me a lot, and I like him too. Maybe I don't want him as much as I want you, but I can work on that. I deserve him, Dylan. I deserve a man who wants to love and cherish me. I deserve a man who sends me a text just to let me know he's thinking of me, who knows my favorite color and why I don't like flowers, and to whom I can reveal my deepest, darkest secrets without fear that he's going to psychoanalyze me."

"Lacey, you can tell me anything. I would love to hear everything about you."

But I didn't want to tell him anything. He already looked at my hands as if they were some problem he'd rather not see. What would he say if he found out I was a liar—and something even worse. No, I'd rather he leave pissed off than look at me with horror or loathing.

I forced the tears to stop, and I steadied the tenuous notes in my voice. "I want you to respect my right to be with Thomas, because he's who I want. He makes me happy."

"Lace—"

"No." I pointed at the door. "No arguments. Leave now and forget tonight happened."

He ground his teeth so hard I heard his jaw pop. "You have no interest in hearing my side of this."

"None."

Whatever explanation he had wouldn't be enough. I've heard it all before.

He left, slamming both my bedroom door and front door on his way out.

I wanted to call him back, to give him another chance, but I managed not to act on that impulse. I meant what I said, and from this day forward, I'm going to respect myself and demand that others treat me accordingly.

Chapter Thirteen

That weekend in Boston, Thomas took me to a fancy restaurant (shocker), but we didn't dine alone. Several of his friends joined us. I met Patrick Westman, the man who let me use his name to book dates for Kiss Me Goodnight. He was there with his partner, and two other couples rounded out the crew.

Thomas and I held hands and laughed, and he stole several small kisses when he thought nobody was looking. I felt guilty about almost sleeping with Dylan, but that feeling evaporated when Thomas refused to identify me as his girlfriend. He introduced me to his buddies and their significant others as his *friend*. They treated me like I was a little more than a friend, but not like I was firmly attached to Thomas. It seemed I was auditioning for the part. Phase one had been the Thomas interview (two dates), and now phase two was meeting the friends. This might continue through the next date, and I suspected phase three involved meeting his mother since we had time to kill before our sexual encounter on the sixth date.

After I thought about it, I appreciated the logic of his approach too much to be offended.

The next weekend, I didn't see Thomas because Kiss Me Goodnight had their first mini-tour. They were playing Cincinnati,

Columbus, Akron, Cleveland, and Ann Arbor: five venues in five days, and I had to go with them. It's amazing how much crap a manager has to do. The band just has to show up, set up, and play. I have to deal with the management and contracts at each venue. They ran my ass ragged, and I earned every cent of what they were paying me, and then some.

Daisy, Gavin, and Levi treated me in the same friendly way they always had. Dylan remained distant, though he was cordial. I sometimes caught him glaring at me. He could pout all he wanted; I wasn't going to change my mind.

Onstage, the band revealed two new songs, which because of my other duties I didn't hear until we were in Akron on the third night. The first one, "Avalanche," featured a haunting melody—who knew Levi also played the violin?—and an angry beat. Dylan's vocals managed to reflect both feelings.

> *The things I do wrong*
> *Pile up like dead snow.*
> *Stale and listless, it covers me,*
> *Overwhelms me,*
> *Consumes me.*
> *Sometimes it seems like I can't catch a break.*
> *I'm damned no matter what I do.*
> *I want to bury myself in that icy grave.*
> *Love doesn't work; it's not for me.*
> *An avalanche seals my fate.*

It has another depressing stanza, and it's a beautiful song. You're going to die when you hear it. I'm sure it'll be one of their biggest hits. Of course, this one, aptly titled "Wrong Name," will be even bigger.

> *The devil in my head*
> *Invaded me in bed.*
> *It made me shout it out—I didn't want to shout—*
> *The wrong name.*
> *I didn't mean it when I said*
> *The wrong name.*
> *Please forgive me when I said*
> *The wrong name.*

I wanted to kill Dylan. He'd made one of the most humiliating moments of my life into a catchy, punk-rock/ska-inspired song that had the audience singing the chorus before he was halfway through. By the end, he just held out the microphone and let them shout the refrain. I was by turns mortified and more pissed than I'd ever been in my entire life.

For the first time ever, I was too upset to even wash my hands. First I wanted to punch Dylan. Then I might calm down enough to freak out and head for the washroom. I paced in the lobby until they finished their set. The moment they completed their signature, self-titled song, I hightailed it back to the dressing room.

I made it there before they did, so I waited in the empty room. It smelled of sweat and body spray, makeup and chemicals. I could hear the four of them laughing and talking as they approached, on a natural high after their performance.

In my sane, rational mind, I knew it had been an incredible concert. They were accruing fans by the hundreds. Their social media following had exploded, and the single we had available for a dollar had over three thousand downloads the last time I checked.

But I'd left rational thought in the dust. I was firmly in downtown Going to Rip Your Face Off.

Dylan was the third person over the threshold. Daisy and Gavin took one look at me, and their heads swung to follow where my laser vision pointed. I marched across the small space — the five of us in there didn't leave much room for moving around — and socked him in the nose. His head snapped back, probably from instinct and astonishment, but I like to think it was because I packed a wallop.

Gavin snagged me around the waist and pulled me away. I didn't fight him because that one hit and the sight of a drop of blood trickling from Dylan's nose sent me straight back to the terror of my childhood. I blacked out.

When I came to, Levi stood over me. They'd set me on one of the folding chairs in the room, and he was doing his best to keep me from falling to the floor.

He grinned when I opened my eyes. "It's good to know you're only capable of a small-scale assault. Tell me, if I ever piss you off that much, can I fake the blood? Will that have the same impact as seeing the real thing?"

I pushed him away and got to my feet.

"Slowly, now. I'll catch you, but I'd still rather you don't keel over again."

Dylan sat on a chair as far away from me as the room would allow. He held an ice cube in a plastic bag to his nose. My pulse leapt. Guilt at what I'd done combined with latent self-loathing to make me feel like a worthless ass. I wanted to throw my arms around him and sob. At the same time, I wanted to punch him again.

One thing I knew for certain: I could not go on this way. This fiasco with Dylan had destroyed my ability to be near him. I snatched a flyer lying on a vanity, scrounged for a pen, and wrote my resignation on the paper. The contract I'd signed had an escape hatch, but it required a fourteen-day notice.

Daisy read over my shoulder. "Lacey, no. You can't quit. We need you. Whatever Dylan did, he can apologize."

"I didn't do anything." He set aside his ice pack and got to his feet. A harsh light darkened his eyes, which weren't circled in black, so I hadn't broken his nose. "I'm not apologizing, but I will accept one."

I felt like punching him again, but I clenched my fists instead. "You didn't do anything? You took the single most humiliating experience of my life and wrote it into a song with a catchy tune."

He shrugged, but that casual gesture didn't diminish the ferocity of his expression. "We already had the music. I just needed the words. Did you want me to dedicate it to you?"

I could take a lot of things, but his sarcasm at that moment wasn't one of them. I was too upset to think of a snappy reply, though I'll probably wake up in the middle of the night with several playing through my head.

Gavin and Levi exchanged looks, and Levi put his arm around me. "Lacey, how about we go back to the hotel and sort this out? There has to be a way we can resolve this without losing you."

I shook my head and swallowed against the burning behind my eyes. I refused to cry in front of Dylan. I wouldn't give him the satisfaction of knowing how deeply he'd hurt me. If my father had taught me nothing else, he'd driven home the point that weakness makes you prey.

"Oh, come on." Dylan jerked my note from Daisy's hand and crumpled it up. "I've been singing that song for three nights, and now you object?"

"This is the first night I wasn't too busy to catch part of your show." Finally calm enough for the motion to be soothing, I rubbed my hands together. "I just knew you guys were impressing the crowds, and that you had some new songs."

Dylan curled his lip and regarded me with undisguised derision. "Maybe if you weren't so busy sexting your newest piece of ass, you'd have heard them sooner."

I didn't want to respond. My relationship with Thomas was none of his business. "You have two weeks to find a new manager. I'll prepare the records and contacts to turn over to whomever you get."

With that, I extricated myself from Levi's arm and exited the room. I had no reason to wait for them, and our hotel was only a block away. I walked to the room I shared with Daisy and washed my hands 102 times.

I had a whole list of calls to return about the band, and I seriously wondered whether I had a duty to do it or not. Some were callbacks from venues I'd been trying to reach to book dates. Others were likely new inquiries. Two were from music company executives who wanted to arrange a date and time to see the band perform. They were very close to landing a recording contract.

It had been a tense two days. Ice formed in a room whenever both Dylan and I were present. The band members were reluctant to get further involved or choose sides, and I didn't blame them. They were a unit, a team, and they'd been friends since long before I entered their lives.

But I'd brought opportunities they wouldn't have had without me, thanks to the contacts I got through Thomas's friend — and my tenacity, of course. I'm sure things would have eventually worked out for them, but I don't deny that my presence expedited the process.

Sunday in Ann Arbor was the closing date for the mini-tour. Kiss Me Goodnight had left the stage, and the crowd thumped around the headliners. Now that it was safe, I headed to the bar to have a drink. Luma and Jane were somewhere in the throng, enjoying a band they liked. I'd touched base with them before the performance, though I hadn't told them anything about that fucking song or my resignation as the band's manager.

"Is this seat taken?"

I looked up from my brooding to find Thomas standing next to me. My troubles slid away, and I launched myself into his arms. He kissed me tenderly and held me close. After this weekend from hell, I needed him more than I ever had.

He guided me back to the stool I'd abandoned at the counter and took the seat next to me. The bar would be packed after the performance, but right now the concertgoers had abandoned it.

"I missed you too."

"You didn't tell me you were flying in. I would have met you at the airport." This gig was close enough to home that I didn't need to be here, which made me wonder why I'd stayed for the performance. Am I a glutton for punishment?

He signaled the bartender and gave his order before turning back to me. "I wanted to surprise you. And I kind of wanted to see this band you're spending all this time managing."

My jaw dropped. "You were here for the performance?"

The bartender delivered his drink. Thomas nodded and sipped. "They're good. Damn good. I'm not a huge fan of alternative music, but I can see the crossover appeal. With the right management, they could get some mainstream play. That song — I think it's called 'Wrong Name' — is priceless. It's ironic and irreverent, catchy without being annoying. They have some good slow songs too. Whoever writes the lyrics must've had his heart broken more than once."

Shoot me in the head. Now, please. I can't take much more of this. I officially hate that song. "Yeah, well, I wish them loads of luck with their next manager."

Thomas frowned. With that goatee, the expression only made him look cuter. "Next manager? Are you quitting? You can't quit. They're good enough to be the next big thing. You've only been with them a short while, but you're the one making that happen."

I shook my head. "I couldn't do any of this without those contacts and Patrick's name. He's your friend, and you're the one who made this possible."

He snorted. "Don't sell yourself short. Patrick didn't give you anything precious. The phone numbers of radio stations and concert venues aren't hard to find. He saved you some legwork, sure, but that's all."

I was poised to disagree, but he barreled on.

"Can you honestly tell me dropping Patrick's name has made a difference? People don't know the names of those who work behind the scenes."

Truthfully, I hadn't used Patrick's name. I'd been sending emails with the band's signature song attached and following up with phone calls and visits. I was pedaling Kiss Me Goodnight like a pharmaceutical rep pedals drugs. And I was also selling liquor at record rates. My two jobs were truly complementary. As it stood, I was scoping out this bar as a possible new client.

Thomas took my silence for agreement. "I thought not. It's you, Lacey. You're an amazing woman. I keep telling you that, and one day you'll finally realize how right I am."

He grinned and smooched my cheek.

"I'm still quitting. I'm not getting along with the lead singer. I punched him a couple of nights ago. That's not good."

Thomas's grin faded, and an ominous light came into his eyes, rendering them a deep, dark brown. "What happened? I thought you two were friends."

"We were. We aren't anymore." I didn't want to say anything else. How could I tell Thomas we'd fought about him, I'd come close to sleeping with Dylan, and then Dylan had written a nasty song about me because he was mad I turned him down? On the other hand, I didn't want to lie to Thomas. I'd begun our relationship like that, but I was determined to be truthful with him.

So I told him everything. Almost everything. I did not tell him I'd intended to sleep with Dylan, though I did admit to the kissing parts. Mostly I focused on how Dylan thought I would wait for him while he spent who knew how many years sorting through his feelings for his deceased wife.

Thomas regarded me soberly. "Do you want to be with him?"

I shook my head. "It was a mistake. He and I are not compatible. I realized that before I ever texted you the photo of those test results. I'm with you because I want to be with you. He just thinks because there was once a bit of 'maybe' between us, he's entitled to having me whenever he decides it's time."

"Wow. When you decide to tell the truth, you really lay it out there, don't you?" He ran his thumb along his jaw as wheels seemed to churn in his head. Thomas is a smart man. He was no doubt reading between the lines and arriving at conclusions. Finally, he closed his hand over mine. "Lacey, you and I are just getting started. Neither of us has stopped dabbling in other options. We've purposely kept things casual because we didn't want to rush. I think the time has come for us to have a serious talk about where we're headed."

"Probably, but I don't want to have it in a bar." I went to slide from my stool. We could go to my place to have this serious talk.

Thomas stopped me. "Wait. I just remembered something Patrick said about working with creative types. Most of them behave like spoiled brats. They're the personality type that seeks the spotlight. They're full of themselves, and they feed on the adoration of fans. But if they weren't like that, they wouldn't work so hard to achieve fame. Don't quit. Give it time. Dylan will move on as soon as he meets another beautiful woman. With his career choice, that won't be long."

I didn't agree with his assessment of Dylan, but I wasn't going to argue the point. "I'll think about it." That's all I would concede. "I have to find Luma and Jane. They want to meet you."

Luma was difficult to peel away from the show until she realized what I wanted. Jane squealed loudly, but she pulled herself together before we made it back to the bar where I'd left Thomas.

He shook the hands of my friends with the enthusiasm of a man who'd spent almost a month hearing about them. I loved my friends more than anything, and Thomas respected their place in my life.

Jane leaned in and gave him a peck on the cheek. "We've heard some pretty spectacular things about you."

He flashed a polite smile, the kind men get when they know they've been dissected by women but aren't sure they want to hear the details. "I can say the same about you and Luma."

I didn't hear everything they said. The band was loud, and once Jane and Luma moved in, I wasn't the closest person to Thomas. But I witnessed laughing and smiles. My friends were being nice, taking in the details of the man who'd flown me to three different cities for dates.

Before too long, Gavin appeared by my side. He'd been letting his hair grow for the first time in his life, and it hung down past his ears. I didn't consider it long, but he did. I guess if you live with a buzz cut for so many years, you forget what it's like to actually have hair. He had that gorgeous blond color with natural highlights for which women pay vast sums of money, and he truly did not appreciate his good fortune.

He hadn't changed after the performance, but since he smelled more like perfume and body spray than manly sweat, I figured he'd been close to female fans. Perhaps Thomas had a point about Dylan; the band did seem to be accumulating groupies everywhere they went. Both Gavin and Levi were single now, so they'd begun to take advantage of their positions in the band.

Gavin slung his arm around my shoulders and pulled me so close his lips brushed against my ear. "Lacey, please don't quit. We can't do this without you."

Politely as I could, I put some space between us. "You can too."

"How about if we kick Dylan out of the band?"

I laughed, but it was a bitter imitation of amusement. "He's your front man and your lyricist. You need him a lot more than you need me. Without me, you'll have to do more work, but without Dylan, you don't have a band."

Thomas must have been shooting a speculative look our way, because Gavin suddenly stuck out his hand. "Gavin Reid. I play bass for Kiss Me Goodnight."

Now that he knew who was hugging on me, Thomas relaxed. He shook Gavin's hand. "Thomas Pritchett. Lacey has mentioned you."

Gavin's handshake stuttered as he no doubt realized he was greeting the man Dylan and I had been fighting about. But he recovered quickly. "Thomas, yes. Lacey says you're the reason she's been able to book us so many shows."

Before Thomas could issue his denial, Gavin continued. "Of course, we all know it has more to do with her persistence and drive than anything else."

The grin on Thomas's face grew tenfold. "I keep trying to tell her that, but as you know, she's stubborn."

That cracked the ice, and the situation thawed considerably. Levi joined us next, and when Daisy and Dylan came our way, they found the six of us raucously conversing at a table on the other side of the bar. That part was abandoned because the stage was obscured from those seats. Lucky us. I can't say I particularly liked the headlining act.

Daisy inserted a chair between Luma and Gavin. Levi and Jane scooted so Dylan could sit as far away from me as possible. That put him in prime position to glare. To be fair, he did split the malice evenly between Thomas and me.

That is, until Levi leaned over and said something short and sharp in his ear. Then Dylan looked everywhere but at me. No matter, I was determined not to let him spoil this unexpectedly good turn on a bad night. My friends had finally met Thomas, and he was charming them all.

Chapter Fourteen

Thomas stayed at my apartment for four days. Turns out he was in Michigan on business. He offered to get a hotel room, but I wouldn't hear of it. I only had one bedroom and one bed, but I was more than willing to share it with him.

We did not have sex.

We also waited until the last morning to have that serious discussion about where our relationship was headed.

We'd stayed up late the night before, talking about tons of different things, and we'd slept in until the need for the bathroom had forced him from the bed. My bladder bowed under the power of my need for fifteen more minutes of sleep.

When I did drag my ass from beneath the covers, I found him eating breakfast. I'd cleared out a second spot at my table/desk for him to use. I think he liked having this evidence that I didn't entertain men at my apartment. He enjoyed reading the newspaper on his tablet while he ate, and I found that habit annoying, so he'd learned to set it aside when I was with him.

The moment I sat down with my bowl of oatmeal, he shut down his tablet and kissed my cheek. "Good morning. You're looking exceptionally lovely today."

I glanced down at my body to see what might have triggered that comment. My boobs weren't showing, but I was wearing a pair of pale gray yoga pants. My ass had probably earned that compliment.

"Thanks. Did you want to talk about where our relationship is headed, or are we going to let that topic alone for at least one more date?" No sense beating around the bush when I could shock him awake faster than coffee.

He laughed and broke his toasted bagel in half. I liked that he didn't seem to feel defensive. I hated having to couch my questions and comments all the time.

"We can talk. Did you want to start?"

I shook my head. "No. You're better at this. You go first."

He cleared his throat, but not in an attempt to put anything off. The man put peanut butter on his bagel—that stuff was sticky. He took a swig of hot coffee to wash it down. "We've been on four dates."

I liked that he didn't count staying with me for four days as a date. He'd taken me, John, and Mom out to dinner the night after he'd arrived. Sharing a meal with my parents also did not count as a date, and he recognized that fact as well. Last night he took just me to a fancy restaurant, and then we spent some time throwing money away at a casino. That counted as a date.

"I think they've gone pretty well. I like spending time with you, and you seem to like spending time with me."

"Oh, yes." I didn't curb my enthusiasm. I did like spending time with him.

"I don't think we're to the part where either of us has fallen in love yet."

"No. We're definitely not there yet." I also liked how he included a qualification, as though he expected it to happen in the future.

He laughed. "I love that you aren't offended by my honest assessment. You're an amazing woman, Lacey. Confident, intelligent, tenacious, beautiful—the complete package."

My package came with a few serious defects that no recall could fix. One of those was a deep suspicion of so many compliments. "Are you seeing someone else?"

"Nope. I've been on a few dates since I've been seeing you, but nobody twice, and nobody since the time you came out to Boston and met some of my friends." He wiped his fingers on his napkin before closing his hand over mine. "Are you seeing anyone else?"

I shook my head. Dylan was nowhere near my radar.

He ran his thumb along my wrist. "Neither of us is seeing anybody else. I propose we keep it that way."

"I second that emotion."

He grinned in acknowledgment of my lame joke. "Motion carried. We are now officially a couple. You may start referring to me as your boyfriend."

I slid the short distance from my chair to his lap, and he closed his arms around me. "Okay, but I still want to wait until the sixth date to sleep together."

He cupped my cheek and guided my face to his. "Whatever you want, honey." Then he kissed me. It was deep and absolute, a display of possession and dominance I never would have expected from Thomas. I thoroughly approved.

An hour later, Thomas had dressed and packed, and I helped him carry his things to my car. We'd returned his rental the day before, after he'd completed his last meeting. I offered to shuttle him to the airport so I could see him off with a proper goodbye kiss.

As we loaded his suitcase in the trunk, I noticed Dylan standing next to his car, staring in our direction.

Thomas noticed him too. "Did you know he was coming?"

I shook my head. "I haven't talked to him since last weekend. You were there."

He made a doubtful sound. "You didn't say a word to him." Nodding in Dylan's direction, he continued, "Do you want me to talk to him?"

The idea that I would let him fight my battles struck me as hilarious. After I finished laughing, I answered him. "Thank you, but I got this one." I tossed him my keys. "Give me a minute to see what he wants."

"All right, but know that I'm here if you need me."

I didn't tell him to start the car in case I assaulted Dylan again and we had to run, but I laughed again at the thought. That's why I had a smile on my face when I made it to where Dylan waited.

Do I even need to tell you how amazing he looked? It galled me that I still noticed after he'd been such a douchebag. And I was officially Thomas's girlfriend. I should not be admiring other men.

He fidgeted as I stopped in front of him, crossing and uncrossing his arms several times before deciding to let them dangle at his sides. "Hey, Lacey. I came by to apologize. I didn't realize you still had company."

Pain flashed through his face, but not so quickly I couldn't catch it. I felt sorry for him, sorry for the opportunities we'd both missed.

"Anyway, I'm sorry. I wrote that song because I was pissed off that you wouldn't listen to me. Then I was pissed off at myself for hurting you." He closed his eyes. When he opened them again, he kept his gaze down. "Sunday night, after I got over myself, I watched you and him together. You're right; he makes you happy. You deserve to be happy. I want that for you."

I wanted it for myself, but I let him have his apology. Everything else aside, he'd become one of my closest friends. The anger billowing my sails went slack, and my fury drained away.

"Thank you. This apology means a lot to me."

He lifted his eyes and ventured a small smile. "Enough to revoke your resignation?"

I stiffened. "Are you here because Daisy, Gavin, or Levi made you come?"

"No. Nobody knows I'm here. Please, Lacey. I don't want to lose your friendship. I can't imagine not having you in my life. These past couple of weeks have been hell."

Yes, they certainly had. I nodded, not sure whether I was agreeing to renew our friendship or manage the band. I opted for the safer choice. "I miss your friendship too."

Dylan wasn't going to let the other matter lie. I didn't blame him. "What about coming back as our manager? We need you, Lace. We really need you."

Again I nodded. "Okay, but I will never like that song."

"Do you want us to stop playing it? Because we will."

Yes. I very much wanted that. However, I couldn't be selfish, not if we were going to make this friendship work. The whole idea of being called the wrong name would eventually be something we laughed about. "No. That's the song people seem to like the most. Thomas loves it. Even after I told him why I hated it, he said it was his favorite."

Dylan's chuckle communicated his discomfort with the topic of Thomas, or maybe with the fact that I'd been so honest with Thomas. "Still, we'll stop if you want."

My heart would eventually harden against the sharp pangs that song induced. Until then, I would rely on my business sense. It tingled, telling me "Wrong Name" would be their first breakout hit. Yes, I had faith that Kiss Me Goodnight would soon become a household name. It's what drove me to pester people until the band got the appearances they needed.

I sighed. "No. Don't get rid of it. But for Pete's sake, you need backing vocals. I'm not kidding, Dylan. We're talking about the difference between people liking KMG and loving it."

He saluted me. "Aye, aye, captain. I will inform Gavin and Levi that they have no choice. If they want you back, they're going to have to contribute vocals."

It was a good way around their reluctance to participate. I shrugged. "You have a show Friday night. We'll have a meeting this afternoon to discuss your set list."

Dylan lifted his chin in Thomas's direction. "Are you sure you're free this afternoon?"

"I'm taking Thomas to the airport. He's heading home today. I have some work to do for my other job, and then I'll stop by Daisy's house."

That seemed to satisfy him, though not completely. Dylan was definitely holding his tongue, which was fine with me. Bald honesty is not always in everybody's best interest.

When I returned to Thomas, he regarded me warily. "He hugged you. Looks like you made up."

"We're friends again, and I've agreed to stay with the band for now."

"Have you?" He frowned.

I was surprised at his reaction. "That's what you told me to do. Since Dylan came here to apologize, I can stay at a job I love, and I saved face. Plus, I'm finally going to get Levi and Gavin to sing. They need backing vocals."

Thomas sighed. "Remind me never to piss you off. You're one hell of a negotiator. Did you get a higher percentage?"

I hadn't asked for one. I threw him my version of a sexy grin. "Next time."

"Next time? You plan to fight with Dylan often?"

I shook my head and pulled out of my parking space. "Dylan and I don't fight often. That was our first real disagreement."

Thomas didn't say anything to that, and I wasn't sure if he shifted uncomfortably or just needed to adjust the placement of his balls. I wondered what he looked like naked. Then I wondered what Dylan looked like, and I shut off that part of my mind. I would eventually train myself not to skip over to Dylan anytime I thought about sex.

I laced my fingers in Thomas's. "I'm going to miss you. I've never had a four-night sleepover before. I like having you around."

Everything I said was the truth, yet it felt a little like a lie.

Two weeks later, after Thomas took me to San Francisco (which he combined with a business trip) for our fifth date, Kiss Me Goodnight reached the milestone of ten thousand paid downloads. And their illegal downloads had gone viral, which didn't bother me. When Levi complained, I reminded him people don't download songs they don't like.

Dylan wrote songs like crazy, producing lyrics to one or two new ones every day. "Wrong Name" was picked up by satellite radio and featured on their college and alternative stations.

I kept busy working my two jobs. In addition to booking shows, I was responsible for the upkeep of KMG's website and social media pages. Daisy and Gavin enjoyed posting status updates and tweets, so I let them have at it, but I did monitor them, and I handled the "official business" postings.

John was doing better. He and my mom had established a routine of daily exercise, and they glowed with health. They also seemed more romantic around each other. My mom had booked a second honeymoon in Hawaii, a place they'd always wanted to visit.

Daisy quit her waitressing job. Dylan cut back on the number of patients he saw. Gavin took a leave of absence, and Levi maxed out his vacation days.

We were to have a meeting today, as it's Thursday and we've formed a habit of meeting every week. Daisy's parents had long ago soundproofed a room in the basement for her to practice the drums, and that's where the magic happened.

I walked in at the end of band practice. They were finishing up a new song.

I know you're thinking of me
In bed
When he's making you scream
And you're biting your lip
To keep
From shouting my name.
You say you love him
But I know you're lying.
I broke your heart
And you wish he was me

The melody was one of those deceptively happy ones. Dylan liked songs where the lyrics were counter to the tone. He loved that The Cure's love songs sounded fatalistic but weren't, and he was infatuated with sixties pop songs that sounded like a celebration of love but were instead about heartbreak.

I was just happy he'd channeled his moodiness into something creative and seemed content to leave me alone. The manager parts of me heard gold in the song.

I clapped as they finished. "That one's a keeper."

Dylan smiled shyly as he stowed his guitar on its stand. "Thanks. It's not quite done. We're tightening up the sound."

The room had a long sofa shoved against one wall, which was piled high with papers and clothes. I moved enough of the mess to sit down and pulled notes from my binder. I gave them a few moments to get themselves settled, and I called the meeting to order.

"First, I've arranged a tour for you. You'll be the opening act for the East Coast leg. There are seventeen dates that span from December to February. I didn't want to commit you to a nationwide tour because we simply don't have the money to pay for transportation and things like that."

Levi stared at me with a deer-in-the-headlights look. I handed him a sheet with the tour dates printed on it. He didn't look. "Lacey,

I'm going to have to quit my job. What happens if this dries up? It doesn't pay as well as my day job. I'm screwed. I'm completely screwed."

I regarded him stoically. The better I got to know Levi, the more I realized how badly he reacted to anxiety. "You're twenty-five years old. Move in with Gavin. Or your parents. It's time to commit to this one hundred percent. Don't freak on me. The items on the agenda only get better."

"How?" Gavin did his best to change the subject. We all wanted to avoid a pity-party/rant-fest courtesy of Levi and his fears of financial insolvency.

I glanced at Dylan. He'd perched his ass on a low stool, and he drummed his fingers on his thighs, his concentration focused on the wall to his left. This would get his attention. "You're opening for AFI."

Yep. He froze, then regarded me wondrously. "You're shitting me."

The grin on my face assured him I was not. "They've heard your music, and they love it. Davey is a huge fan."

It was weird to say his name out loud with people in the room. I'd whispered/moaned it in the privacy of my bedroom often enough. I couldn't believe I was going to meet the man for whom I'd named my vibrator. Holy cow, what if he was a jerk and meeting him ruined my fantasies forever? I'm not sure I could survive it. I mean, I still had Jared and Simon, but they weren't Davey.

The silence in the room testified to the level of shock. This was a band they idolized.

"Lacey," Gavin said, "I want to kiss you."

Dylan shot him a black look. "She has a boyfriend."

Daisy laughed. "He was kidding."

Not wanting to continue down this road, I resumed the discussion. "Also, you have inquiries from three recording companies. Do you have a preference for who you want to meet and when? Or do you want to go indie and cut the tracks yourself?"

I outlined the companies and my research on each. The meeting went on for another hour, falling apart when Monty arrived from track practice. He was starving, and Daisy wanted to have dinner ready when Audra got home.

We hadn't resolved anything. I felt like making an executive decision, but I couldn't. Whether to go with an established company or go it alone wasn't a choice I could make for them. My job was to manage the choices they made.

Dylan walked me outside. Our relationship had changed a lot in the last couple weeks since we'd established a safe, neutral zone, and our friendship flourished. "Gavin and I are taking Monty bowling tonight. Want to come?"

I threw my bag into the backseat of my car. "I haven't been bowling in forever. I suck."

He shrugged. "On a good day, I can bowl a one-forty. I'm no pro bowler either. It's just for fun. Monty's going to kick all our asses anyway."

"Can Luma come? I'm supposed to hang out with her tonight." I knew Luma wouldn't mind bowling with the guys. I suspected she was developing a crush on Gavin. She still said she only liked African-American men, but I didn't believe her.

"Sure. Thomas isn't in town?"

I shook my head. We had our sixth date scheduled for this weekend, and I was nervous as hell about sleeping with him. I hadn't been with a real man in more than two years.

"I'll see him Saturday. He's flying me to Hartford." I'd see his house for the first time. Opening the driver's side door, I threw my purse across to the passenger side. The seat was littered with junk from both jobs. "I'll call Luma. Text me the when and where, and I'll see you there."

Dylan grinned and held the door while I got inside. "Rhymes like that are why *I* write the lyrics."

As I drove away, I reflected on how much I liked the way our relationship had changed. Undercurrents of "what if" were gone. I no longer wondered if he was going to kiss me or make a move. I knew he wouldn't, though I wasn't always so sure about myself. The electricity between us hadn't lessened, but I was a champion at ignoring it.

I'd be lying if I said I didn't regularly check him out, though. I couldn't help it. When that much hotness is thrust into your face, I dare you not to look.

Chapter Fifteen

When Luma and I arrived at the designated place, we immediately got lost. The bowling alley I'd been to a handful of times growing up had eighteen lanes. This one boasted two hundred, and they were all in full swing. The place smelled of leather and sweat, and it was jam-packed with people.

Dylan finally found us near the entrance and led us to a counter where a woman with exactly one tooth in her lower jaw asked for my shoe size. Or at least, I think that's what she wanted. After deciding I wasn't sure, I asked, "What?"

The song blaring over the loudspeaker was temporarily suspended while someone at the grill informed lane 157 that their chili dogs were ready for pickup.

Dylan coughed and leaned against the counter. "What's your shoe size?"

"Seven."

He shouted my answer to the woman. She nodded and threw a pair of tattered bowling shoes onto the plastic-coated surface. Something inside me recoiled at wearing shoes that had housed thousands of sweaty feet before mine.

Luma of the Munchkin Feet asked for a size five. She carried both pairs of shoes as we followed Dylan past a lot of colorful people. By colorful, I mean their tattoos. Their clothing was mostly black, which highlighted the colors swirling on arms and legs, peeking from the necks of shirts, and creeping up to decorate places where hair used to be. I wanted to stop and study, turn up the lights so I could see everything better.

I stared so much that Dylan put his arm around my waist to keep me moving. He leaned down to admonish me. "Lacey, people don't like to be stared at."

"But it's so pretty. I think I'm a little turned on."

He stumbled, taking me with him, but he recovered for both of us. "I have a tattoo."

My full attention snapped to him. I'd seen him shirtless and in shorts, but I hadn't seen any body art. "Where?"

A shit-eating smile curled the corner of his mouth. "Secret."

Oh, Lord. Do not tell me he has ink on his dick. I'm not sure how I feel about that. "Did it hurt?"

"Of course it hurt. It's a tattoo. I'm thinking of getting one on my arm. Something cool to ring my bicep."

It took an act of will to not drool. "What is it?"

"I don't know. I haven't seen what I want. I might design it myself."

"I meant the one on your ass."

He grinned. "I never said it was on my ass."

"Upper thigh?"

His grin didn't go away, but his arm tightened around me, and he feathered his fingers along my hip. I noticed the move, but I didn't draw attention to it. "I said it's a secret. You'd have to see me naked."

Luma snorted, reminding us we weren't alone. I walked dangerously close to the edge by flirting with Dylan.

I removed his hand from my hip. "Some other time, then. Can you tell me what it is?"

He also dropped his coy demeanor. "It's a rosebud, and it has my parents' initials in it. Daisy has a matching one. We got them when our parents died."

That's so sweet. I wondered if he also had something to commemorate his late wife.

We finally made it to the lanes they'd reserved. Gavin threw me an ugly button-down shirt. "You're on Dylan's team. Luma and I are going to clean the lanes with your sorry asses."

I hadn't known there'd be teams. Monty was also on our team, as were three people I didn't know. Four additional people—all strangers to me—rounded out Gavin's team. The twelve of us had two lanes.

Dylan shrugged into a shirt matching the one Gavin tossed me.

"I programmed your names into the scoring machine already," Gavin said. "You're late, so we used up your practice shots."

"Hey," Luma protested.

Monty cruised up to the table, put down a huge plastic cup with a red-and-brown swirl of frozen soda inside, and leaned on Dylan's shoulder. "You snooze, you lose. If you hadn't shown up now, we'd be fighting over who got to take your turns."

I looked to Dylan for confirmation. He shrugged. "It's true. Put on your bowling shoes, ladies, and prepare to lose."

"We're on the same team," I reminded him.

"Oh, right. In that case, hurry up. It's your turn."

I truly did not want to put those shoes on my feet. Dylan must have interpreted my expression to mean I'd be in the bathroom all night washing my hands if I had to touch them. He knelt on the floor, removed my shoes, and replaced them with the rented ones.

For ten full seconds, I seriously considered switching from washing my hands incessantly to washing my feet.

Because he was so close, I leaned forward to say something without anybody overhearing. I caught the scent of his spicy aftershave mixed with whatever he'd used on his hair.

"Dylan?"

He still had my foot propped against his knee. Without glancing up, he said, "Yeah?"

"Thank you for putting all that business behind us. I like having you as a friend."

His hand paused on my ankle, and he lifted his gaze to meet mine. I expected an apology, but all I got was a bit of a cocky smirk.

"I haven't put anything behind me. This thing you have with Thomas will never work out. You're from different worlds. You have very different interests and very little chemistry. There's nothing holding you together but your stubbornness and his discerning eye. You're a very beautiful woman, definitely arm-candy material."

I gaped at him, stunned. "I have feelings for Thomas, and he has feelings for me."

He shrugged. "You like him, but that's all. It's very platonic." Then he leaned closer, and his lips almost brushed my ear. "I notice everything about you, Lace. The way your breathing speeds up when I'm this close to you. The way you undress me with your eyes. One day you'll figure out you can't fight fate."

With my palm planted firmly on his chest, I pushed him away. "I don't believe in fate."

That was not a lie. If fate existed, I must have done some pretty horrible things in a past life. Dylan finished with my shoes, but his superior look didn't diminish.

We began bowling, and I performed as expected: two gutter balls in a row. I was off to a rocking start. Monty shook his head, and Luma outright razzed me. The seven strangers didn't comment, which was good. They didn't know me. It was polite to wait until I was out of earshot before denigrating my character.

The next time my turn came around, Dylan went with me. He walked me through the approach, what to do with my arms, and how to aim. His demeanor had reverted back to friendly, and I was grateful. I could almost pretend he'd never said those things to me. After knocking down my first pin, I whiffed the second attempt.

Gavin poured me a beer from the community pitcher. "Here. This might improve your aim."

I accepted the cup. "It certainly can't hurt."

It took a few frames, but I did eventually manage to hit one or two pins consistently. Once I even got nine, but I'd stumbled at the line and fallen on my ass, so that score was due more to providence—not fate—than the emergence of talent. The two cups of beer I consumed on an empty stomach were likely a factor as well.

I ended the first game with a score of 45. Luma got 98. Gavin and Dylan both came in over 135, and Monty bowled 203. Dylan had said the kid was going to win.

As we waited between games for people to raid the grill and get refills on the beer, I sat next to Dylan and willed my head to stop spinning.

"I need to eat."

"I know. I sent Luma and Gavin over to get you something. Why didn't you tell me you hadn't eaten?"

I shrugged. "I wasn't hungry."

My lips felt tingly. I knew it was from the alcohol, but with Dylan sitting next to me looking and smelling so invitingly masculine, I had trouble convincing my mouth it didn't want to be connected to Dylan's. *He isn't right about my relationship with Thomas*, I told myself. *He can't be.*

As I wrestled with the demons of attraction, I noticed a man a few lanes down. Medium height, tubby in the middle, ink-covered arms, and yellow button-down shirt. The shirt drew my attention. He was the only one in two lanes, and his friends hadn't left in pursuit of food and beverages; they'd never been there. He was playing both lanes himself.

As I watched, he held the ball in his hands and brought it close to his face. Then his lips moved. He spoke to it, whispering who-knew-what. Then he puckered up and smacked his lips right on that ball.

"He's kissing his balls."

Dylan looked at me funny. "What?"

"That man." I indicated without pointing or looking directly.

It took Dylan a few moments to cull him from the crowd. "Yellow shirt?"

"Yep. Watch him. He kisses his balls."

Sure enough, he did it again. I giggled. I couldn't help myself. Dylan tried to suppress his laughter, but the more I pealed, the harder he had to fight. I laughed so hard that people stared, and I almost toppled onto the floor. Dylan grabbed my arm to keep me seated.

Monty returned. He gave me the same look Dylan had. "What's wrong with her?"

I motioned him closer. What I had to say needed to be whispered. "That man is kissing his balls."

First he looked at me like I was crazy. Then he turned to find I was speaking the truth. He snorted. "Lacey, you're funny. I like you. When you and the old man here get married, I'm going to hang at your house a lot."

That sobered me. I looked to Dylan for an explanation, but he merely flashed that same cocky smirk and shrugged. I was on the verge of telling him to set Monty straight when my phone rang. As it was my mother, I picked up.

"Hey, Mom. What's up?"

The sound of balls hitting pins, the laughter and chatter of patrons, and the music blaring over the speakers made her impossible to hear. I couldn't make out what she said. Everything seemed garbled. Immediately my anxiety level went through the roof.

"Hold on, Mom. Let me get to a quieter place." I looked around, but there were people everywhere. Quiet bowling alleys were found only on ESPN.

I hurried toward the entrance and stepped outside. I hoped to hell she'd called to convince me to have German chocolate cake with her and not tell John. "Okay, go ahead."

Not garbled. She was crying — sobbing and hiccupping. "It's John. He went to take a nap. We walked three miles this morning, and we were both feeling a little tired. When I woke up, he was cold. Lacey, John died."

Strength drained from my knees. My joints turned liquid. Everything turned liquid. My mother must be in shock because normally she breaks bad news to me gently. John was the love of her life. She had to be devastated. She needed me. I needed her. I couldn't move or speak.

I looked up to find Dylan and Luma standing over me. They said things I couldn't hear. Luma disappeared. So did my shoes.

I have vague memories of Luma and Dylan loading me into a car, but that's all. When I woke the next morning, I was in my old room at my mother's house. Mom was asleep next to me. The two of us were crunched into a twin-size bed. I was a little sore, but I wasn't sure why.

Rolling gently so I could leave without waking my mom, I took stock of my aches and pains. The pounding in my head and my stuffy sinuses indicated I had cried hard. I didn't remember. This hadn't happened to me since I was little. I used to cry a lot for no reason, mostly in my sleep.

"Lacey?"

Oops. I tried to apologize, but sounds wouldn't come out of my mouth.

"Where are you going?"

I pointed at the door to the bathroom.

"Okay, sweetheart. I sent Luma to your place last night. She packed a bag for you. We were thinking you should stay here for a little while."

John had been everything to us. In the dark days after that whole thing with my father, he'd saved us both. First, he'd been my counselor. I'd played in his office every day, never speaking a word.

To my mother, he'd been the man who swept her off her feet and saved her daughter's sanity. He was the one who'd renamed me. Until him, I'd been Alice. One day when he was making lunch for us, he said, "Lacey, would you like to try this Asian sesame dressing on your salad?"

I said, "Yes."

It was a stunning moment for everybody. I hadn't uttered a sound in two years. Most people had stopped talking to me. They behaved as if I were deaf as well as silent. Not John. Never John. He talked to me every day, included me in everything.

From that moment on, Alice was dead. I was Lacey. Always and irrevocably Lacey.

Later, John confessed to my mom that he'd misspoken. But in tripping over his tongue, he'd made me a new person, and gave me another chance at life.

And now he was gone.

My heart was broken.

I couldn't speak, but I knew I would. I had to. For him.

I nodded at my mother. Staying at her house would enable me to be there for her. She'd lost her husband, the only man she'd ever loved. Years ago, she'd confessed to me that her relationship with my father had been a fling. Conceiving me had been an accident—one she didn't regret, but not something she'd planned.

But John? He was the real deal.

The moments of the day sifted through my consciousness, seeming to last forever and be over much too quickly. People visited. Some of them hounded us to eat. We weren't hungry.

Later that evening, after the people had gone, I sat in the living room with Mom. Sadie lay curled on the sofa in John's spot, waiting for him to scoot her to the side so he could sit too. Neither of us sat in his place. I know we both hoped he'd walk in at any moment, and we'd awaken from this nightmare.

"Mom? Why did you wait until after eight o'clock to call me? You said you guys had taken a nap."

She blushed. "Well, we worked out a bit before taking a nap, and that exhausted us. I slept until about seven thirty." Her eyes took on that faraway look, only laced with pain. "I tried to wake him. I was going to tease him about sleeping so late."

Tears tracked down her cheeks. She'd held them in for most of the day, being strong because she didn't like to cry in front of others. "Lacey, how am I going to live without him?"

I didn't know how to answer that.

The next morning, Daisy and her family came over. Audra and Monty cleaned the house. Mom wanted to have the wake here, but neither of us had the energy to focus on a specific task. Daisy helped Luma and Jane make the phone calls my mom wanted made.

Dylan didn't leave my side. He sat on the sofa next to Sadie and watched me as I paced or talked to people. He was a sentinel when I froze, staring into space as if I could find John between molecules of air. He didn't say much, but having him here helped.

Thomas came that evening. I didn't recall talking to him or texting him about John's passing. He took me in his arms and held me for the longest time.

"Jane said you weren't in a good state."

All things considered, I thought I was doing okay. Except for that first morning, I hadn't lost my ability to speak or interact with my surroundings.

"I'm okay," I said. "I'm doing better."

I don't know when Dylan left, only that when I looked up next, he was gone.

Chapter Sixteen

The funeral was beautiful. Daisy, Audra, Luma, and Jane decorated the chapel at the funeral home with collages of John. I spent hours studying the board with pictures of him as a child, and then I got stuck on the pictures he'd taken when he and my mom first got together.

I looked so haunted, a ghost of a child who neither smiled nor spoke. I had mittens on my hands to keep me from washing the skin off. I remember wanting so badly to die. If I could've rewound time to make things different, I would have. Then, I would have. Not now.

Because John had come into my life, I learned that fathers weren't evil. I learned that I didn't have to be glued to my mother's side at all times to feel safe. I realized life was worth living, and I was not the worthless piece of shit my father had labeled me.

Grief made my bones weak. I rocked forward, and a strong arm came around my waist to prop me up. "Let's get you settled. They're going to start the service in a few minutes."

I leaned against Dylan, soaking up his strength because I'd used my reserves.

The service was long. My mother had a minister there to give the sermon, and then she opened the floor for anybody who wanted to talk about John. We were there for three hours. I listened to people, some of whom I'd never met, talk about John's generous nature and loving soul. Some of them addressed my mom and me directly. Others sobbed as they spoke.

I wanted to go to the dais and tell everybody what he'd done for me. It was something we'd kept private, a process only my mom and I were privy to. Now I wanted the world to know how extraordinary he was.

The minister, a woman who appeared to be around my age, helped me up the two steps and positioned me behind the podium. She hovered nearby, and I had to wonder if I looked that bad. Why did people keep thinking I was going to keel over?

I saw Thomas sitting in the row behind mine. Dylan and my friends from the band sat on the other side of the aisle. All the chairs were filled, and people lined the back and sides of the room.

"I can see by the sheer number of people here today that John touched many lives. He was a wonderful man and a remarkable person. There was nothing he loved more than helping people. He was a one of those rare people who gave of himself to everybody."

I paused to sniffle, and I had to wave the minister away. No doubt she hadn't realized the service was going to take so long.

"When I met John, I was a mess. Bad things had happened in my life, and I'd withdrawn from the world. I couldn't speak, and I wouldn't interact with anybody but my mom. I wanted to die."

One deep breath to banish the images that threatened to overwhelm me, and I continued.

"John helped me see it wasn't my fault. He helped me accept what happened and how it had changed me. He made me see that life was worth living, and that I deserved to be loved. I put that man through a lot—him and my mom—but he never blamed me for it. He never made me feel like a burden. I never called him 'father,' because he was so much more than that to me."

By the time I finished, my mom was at my side. She held my hand tightly, and I stayed there with her while she talked about losing her best friend, her lover, and her husband.

Flecks of blood dotted the backs of my hands, and I turned them over to reveal smears where I'd tried to wipe it away. I looked up at the people who still milled around after the service, and I knew I was the only one who could see it. Nonetheless, I excused myself to the bathroom.

I washed, scrubbing at the stubborn spots that wouldn't come clean. As I did, echoes of my stepmother's screams rang in my ears, and I felt myself sliding backward. Years of progress fell away. I shrank. My body was that of a six year old again.

I'd crawled out of bed early because I had to use the bathroom. The house was dark, so I was careful to be quiet. My father had a temper, and I hated doing anything to set him off. My visits were so much nicer when he was in a good mood.

My stepmother, Kathy, often put him in a good mood. She was magic, able to take him from furious to apology with one soft look. A year before, she'd given him a son. I'd fallen in love with Jason before he was born. The idea of having a little brother tickled my fancy like nothing else. Kathy let me help her decorate the nursery, and she often left Jason with me while she went into the kitchen to make lunch or dinner.

Noises from Jason's room drew my attention. It was too early for him to wake up. My father would be upset. He wasn't a morning person. I crept closer. I could soothe my brother back to sleep. I'd done it before. Kathy told me all the time what a good big sister I was, how much Jason loved me.

His door opened suddenly, and Dad's large form stumbled into the hall. He wiped his palm on his shirt. I pressed my body to the wall, hiding in the shadow behind the potted fake ficus next to a hutch. If he didn't see me, he wouldn't get mad at me for waking Jason. I hadn't meant to.

He disappeared back into his room, and I stole into Jason's. Sometimes he fell asleep a little, and then he would start awake. If he found himself alone, he would cry. He was learning to say my name. It didn't sound like much, but he was trying. Sometimes he'd get so excited he'd grab my lips and squeeze as he squealed. It hurt, but I didn't mind. He didn't do it to be mean.

I hoisted myself up to bend over the railing. I couldn't see him clearly, so I stroked my hand down his back. It came away wet and sticky. Jason hated being wet. I knew how to change his diaper. Kathy let me help her all the time.

I climbed down and lowered the railing. When I reached for him, I realized he was soaking. I needed to see the extent of the damage. How could Dad not notice Jason was so wet? He was going to get a rash all over if I left him like that.

Jason had a nightlight, so I closed his door as quietly as I could and turned it on. In the dim light, I could see that the wetness coating him was too dark. A sense of dread wrapped its hand around my heart and squeezed. I wanted to whisper his name, but I knew it wouldn't do any good. His pajamas — a polar bear pattern I'd picked out for him — were shredded, and he lay on his stomach, his cheek bathed in a pool of blood. My stomach roiled, threatening to get sick.

Blood was all over the place, covering his little body, his arms that had hugged me so tight last night before bed, the mattress, the wall behind the crib…and me. It was all over me. I looked down at my hands, staring at the splatters and specks with horror. Red smears marked the front of my nightgown where I'd pressed it against the crib rails.

This was my little brother's blood. Jason was dead. He wasn't pretending. Babies didn't know how to pretend like this.

Screams came from down the hall. "Bill! What are you doing? No! Don't! Please!"

Panic pushed me down, and I rolled under the crib, wedging myself in the corner farthest from the door. It went on like that for a long time, her screams punctuating the horrible stillness in the room.

Jason's blood dripped down through gashes in the mattress, landing on me. It smelled tinny. I tried wiping them away, but it only smeared. Kathy's screams grew weak. I clutched in the semidarkness, searching for something. I knew I should go to help her, but I was too afraid to move.

My groping hand found cold metal. Dad's gun. Dad kept his guns underneath Jason's crib, where he said nobody would ever look for them.

I was frightened of guns. Dad had once taken me out into the backyard when he practiced with his targets. The report was loud, and I hated the sound, but I'd pretended not to mind so much. If he found out I was afraid, he'd make me watch him every time I came over, and he'd make fun of me.

Kathy's screams had stopped, and that terrified me more than the guns.

A door opened down the hall. "Alice? I know you're not sleeping."

He was in my room. I gripped the handle of the gun tightly and wished so hard to be with my mom.

The door to Jason's room opened. Dad came in. "Alice, where are you?"

No sound came out of my mouth, not even a whimper. If I stayed where I was and didn't make a noise, he would leave. I knew he would.

Except he didn't. He came closer, his shadow even larger in the dimness of the nightlight.

"Alice, I know you're hiding under the bed. Come out, sweetheart. Daddy has a surprise for you."

I saw the light glint on the knife in his hand. It was huge, covered with Kathy's and Jason's blood. He was going to kill me too.

Without thinking, I hoisted the gun and pulled the trigger. The roar hurt my ears. It wasn't like on television in those movies my father liked to watch. It was louder—much, much louder. I heard a ringing. It resonated deep in my skull. My father's body crumpled, and I squeezed my eyes shut. Curled in that corner, I waited in silence, the tangy scent of blood and death permeating the air.

Hands pulled me from under the bed, and when I fought to get back, they tightened like iron bands, pinning my arms to my torso. I couldn't move. I couldn't breathe.

"Close your eyes, Lacey. Concentrate on the sound of my voice. Picture the way the stars looked over the water when I took you to the river. Take one breath. Slowly. You're here with me. Be in this moment."

I did as I was told. Gradually, I caught my breath. The room wavered. The sights and smells of my brother's room faded. I was in the bathroom at the funeral home, and Dylan had wrapped his body around mine. We were on the floor.

I wondered how hard I'd fought him. "Did I hurt you?"

He exhaled hard, a whoosh of air that released the tension running through his body, but he didn't let me go. "No, but I might have hurt you. I'm sorry. You may have some bruising. You're quite a fighter."

"John used to call me that."

"A fighter?" Dylan lifted his leg from where it pinned mine. "I don't doubt it. After what you've been through…only a fighter could survive."

In my speech, I'd stuck to generalities. "You have no idea what I've been through."

He relaxed his arms and sat us up, but he didn't let me go. "You don't remember what you were saying as you washed your hands, do you?"

I hadn't been speaking. I'd been stuck in a memory loop, something that hadn't happened to me for years. "I didn't say anything." The silence always protected me.

"Oh, Lacey."

The pain in his voice shot straight to my core. Slowly, I turned in his arms, my body sliding until it was pressed sinfully against his. The teal in his eyes had darkened, edging more toward blue. I hated the misery I saw there, and I knew pity waited in the background.

I tasted his lips once to banish the misery. Twice to obliterate the pity. Three times because I loved him, and I was too tired to fight it.

He kissed me back, and I felt the wonder of his hands playing along my back and moving up to cup my face. When he tangled his fingers in my hair, I was lost. I wanted him with a vicious intensity — right there, right then. I loosened his tie and tore at his shirt. My Dylan wore concert T-shirts and jeans, not dress shirts and ties. He pried my hands loose, and I let him because having him barechested wasn't enough. I wanted him naked and inside me.

When I felt for his cock to bring it to life, he captured my hands again and held them behind me. "Lacey, no. Not here. Not like this. Not with your boyfriend waiting in the lobby outside."

His refusal washed over me, hitting me hard in the gut. Shame tasted bitter in my mouth.

I got to my feet and fixed my clothes. "I'm sorry."

That was a lie. I wasn't sorry. I still wanted him to take me hard and fast against the bathroom wall.

He retucked his shirt and tightened his tie. "I am too. For everything." He hesitated, his hands spread wide as if he wanted to say something more, but I think he knew words were futile just now. He escorted me from the room, and we parted ways. I found my mom sitting with John's sister. I sat down next to her and put my head on her shoulder.

Running to Thomas wouldn't have been fair to him, not with my emotions a morass of need and want and pain. But I saw him a lot as the hours dragged on. Once we'd transferred to the wake at my mom's house, he stayed mostly with Luma and Jane, but he was never far from me.

Chapter Seventeen

Thomas took me home after the wake and put me to bed. When I woke in the morning, I found him asleep on the sofa. I perched on the edge and touched his arm gently. He shifted, turning onto his back and stretching before opening his eyes.

"Good morning."

He scrubbed a hand over his face. "Morning. Did you sleep okay?"

"Yeah. You didn't have to sleep out here. This couch isn't nice to necks." Plus, he had only a thin blanket. He'd slept in sweatpants and a college T-shirt, and his arm was frosty where I touched it.

He sat up, folded the blanket, and slung it over the back of my sofa. "Lacey, you and I need to talk."

His tone left no doubt in my mind that it was a talk I didn't want to have. "How about breakfast? I can make you cheesy eggs and toast. The coffee is already brewing."

As if to punctuate my point, water hissed and spit on the heating elements of my coffeemaker.

"Thanks, but I'd better not. What I have to say won't take long. I just didn't want to say it yesterday. I feel like an ass for saying it today, but leaving it for another day will just make things uncomfortable between us."

"Thomas…" I dreaded days like this. As many times as I've been dumped, you'd think I'd be used to it. I also loathed being on the other side of this equation.

"Dylan is in love with you. That fact has been blatantly clear from the start. I thought it was a one-way thing, but recent events have forced me to face the fact that it's not. You're in love with him."

My chest heaved as I struggled to contain the grief. I folded my hands on my lap. "I want to be in love with you."

He laughed, but it was potent with unhappiness. "That explains a few things."

In the harsh morning light, my stubborn nature had returned. I wish it had brought my better sense with it. "Please give me another chance."

"No. Lacey, I don't want to be your second choice. I don't doubt that you like me, and you wish you had stronger feelings for me. But you can't force it."

This wasn't fair. I tried so hard to fall in love with Thomas. "Dylan doesn't love me. He wants to use me to replace his wife."

Thomas narrowed his eyes and stroked his beard. I loved his scruffy morning face. It made him seem less perfect and more attainable. Just now, I realized it was an illusion. He'd never been perfect. He'd never tried to be or tried to convince me he was. Dylan had been right: Thomas is from a different world, and I would never truly fit in. Every time we ate together, I concentrated on using the right silverware instead of enjoying the food and his company. He thought nothing of flying me somewhere for a night on the town, and I could count the number of non-Thomas-related trips I'd taken on one hand.

Thomas cupped my cheeks in his hands. "You're mistaken. His songs are about you. All of them. Every time you send me a new recording, it smacks me across the face with how blatant he is."

"Thomas, please. I don't want to talk about him. I want to know how I can fix this. I never wanted to hurt you."

He kissed my cheek, a brotherly peck that put us firmly back at square one. "I believe you. That's why I didn't sleep in your bed, and it's why I waited until this morning to talk to you. I'm going to get dressed and head out."

When he was ready, I walked him to the door. He had a rental car waiting in the parking lot. Along with procuring an airline ticket, it was another arrangement he'd made while I was sleeping.

I wanted to hug him, but I was afraid he'd mistake it for desperation. I was resigned now. "I hope you find someone who loves you the way you deserve to be loved."

"Thanks." He turned to leave, but at the last second, he pulled me to him for a tight hug. "I'm not mad at you, and I don't blame you, so don't punish yourself for this, okay?"

I nodded, a small lie that made him feel better. Unfortunately, it rekindled the urge to lie I'd been suppressing for months. And I no longer had the desire to fight it.

After breakfast, I called my mom to see what her plans were. It was weird how I had no problem butting into her life like this. I couldn't remember ever calling for her daily itinerary, but then again, John had always been there.

"I'm going to lunch with some of my friends, and then John's sisters want to come over for dinner. You're welcome to come with me, sweetie, but you don't have to."

I liked my mother's friends and John's sisters, but I didn't feel much like company. "Thanks, but I'm going to get some work done. I haven't done anything since last week."

The list of messages on my cell was enormous, and most of them had to do with the band. I got to work.

Several hours later, Dylan called. I answered, even though I knew I shouldn't. The mood I was in…let's just say things could get ugly. Burying myself in work was the best treatment for my problem.

"Hey. I wanted to see how you're doing."

My stomach gurgled. I'd skipped lunch. "I'm hungry. Can you bring me some soup?"

He chuckled, the nervous kind. "Ask Thomas to get you some soup. He's there to take care of you."

I waved my hand dismissively even though he couldn't see it. "We broke up. He went home."

"He broke up with you?" Iron fury underlined his words.

"Yes."

Dylan swore and called Thomas some creative names. "Are you alone?"

"Yes, and Dylan? It was really a very amicable breakup. I'm not angry with him." He hadn't been the one making out with someone else in the bathroom at John's funeral. I wasn't proud of my behavior.

Dylan did not address my point. "What kind of soup?"

"Doesn't matter. I'm hungry. I'll eat almost anything."

The soup ended up being white bean chili. I love chili, and the weather had taken a turn toward fall. There's nothing more fulfilling than a steaming bowl of chili in the fall.

"Audra made it two days ago. It's vegetarian, so it should still be good."

He sat across from me, in the spot I'd cleared for Thomas. I didn't sit in my usual place, choosing instead to clear a third seat. One day I would have a proper office and a clear dining table.

I spooned chili into my mouth and almost fainted from sheer pleasure. Once I swallowed, the heat crept up on me. My eyes watered, and I coughed. Dylan got me a glass of milk. When the smoke cleared, he sat once again in the same chair, his hands folded on the table as he watched me eat.

He looked delicious in his plain black cotton T-shirt and jeans. The chain connecting his wallet to his belt was back in place. He hadn't worn it in a while. The dark hair falling over his forehead made him look boyish, though the intense expression on his face negated that effect.

"You're not having any?" There was plenty. He'd shoved a plastic dish full of it into my refrigerator.

"I already ate."

I felt the need to spin a tale. To stave off that urge, I grasped at anything. "Dylan, I want to hear your side of the story. Why did you call me Nadia when you were kissing me?"

He looked away from me for the longest time. The tips of his ears turned pink, so I wasn't going to force the issue. If he'd changed his mind and our ship had sailed, at least I'd know exactly where I stood with him. Deep down, I harbored hope he wasn't going to pretend I hadn't asked the question. As I waited, I tried to ignore the urge to wash my hands.

Finally, he cleared his throat. "Habit, mostly. And guilt. There I was, about to make love to an incredible woman, and…" He trailed off, biting his lip as he thought. "I met Nadia when I was nineteen, and she was twenty. She was exciting and smart, always on the go. We were married three months later. She's the only woman I've ever been with."

It took a minute for his point to penetrate. "You were a virgin when you met her?"

The idea of Dylan keeping his virginity intact beyond the age of fifteen or sixteen seemed far-fetched to me.

"Yeah. I was fourteen when Daisy got pregnant. I've played the role of really involved uncle since before I turned fifteen. It was just the three of us for a long time, and I truly did not want to take the chance I'd have a kid before I was ready. I saw firsthand how hard it's been for Daisy. So, I waited."

I knew if I told him I thought it was sweet that he'd waited, he'd never finish his story.

"The morning before she went out backcountry skiing, we fought in our room at the lodge. I told her I wanted a divorce. She called me names, stormed out, and that's the last time I saw her alive. I didn't want to be married to her anymore, but I didn't want her to die."

I read the guilt in every line of his body. "It wasn't your fault."

"I know, but that doesn't make me feel less responsible. I keep thinking if she hadn't been so pissed at me, she would've been more aware of her surroundings. Or maybe if we hadn't fought, we would've spent the morning snuggled under the covers, and she never would have gone backcountry skiing. I wasn't as good as her; I never would've attempted a trek like that. Then part of me thinks she only went to piss me off."

Using a piece of bread, I sopped up the last bits of chili. This helped me avoid looking too closely at Dylan and making him feel more self-conscious. "Why would you think she wanted to piss you off?"

He made motions with his hands, waving air toward him as if the increased oxygen would aid in finding the words he sought. "Daisy never liked Nadia. She thought Nadia wanted to control me, that she wanted everything in the relationship to be about her. Kiss Me Goodnight is the third band I've formed. Nadia resented the time I spent with the other two, and my absence eventually broke them up."

"But you told me she was a proponent of pursuing your dreams."

"*Her* dreams. She wanted me to support her dreams. It took me so long to get through school because she resented the time it took away from her. I didn't even want to go skiing. I wanted to go cage diving with sharks or zip lining, but we always did what she wanted. Before we left, Daisy reminded me that sometimes relationships don't work out, and divorce didn't mean I was a failure. She said there was somebody out there fated to be with me."

Dylan was a romantic. I never would have imagined that. And it sounded like Daisy was right when she told me he'd been over Nadia before she died. I wanted to be naked and next to him so badly I ached. Help me, but Thomas had hit the nail on the head: I loved Dylan with every fiber of my being, and hearing his explanation only made me love him more.

Yet, I knew I couldn't be the person out there who was right for him. I'm too cynical. My life experiences have jaded me to the point where I don't believe in fate like he does—although maybe he could make me believe in magical things again. No, more than likely, I'd eventually ruin everything and break his heart. Am I more afraid of being happy or of doing something to make Dylan leave?

I resisted the urge to move closer to him. "I'm pregnant."

A sharp intake of breath conveyed his shock. "Did you tell Thomas?"

"Yes. He said he'd pay for the abortion, but I can't do that." Now that I'd started, there was no end in sight. Dylan had better take this hint to heart and move on with his life. "I'm going to have the baby. He came into the bathroom last night and saw us kissing. He wants nothing to do with me or the child, so I'm going to do this alone."

"Lacey—" Dylan clenched his fist.

"He's very wealthy, and he's looking for someone who has more in common with his lifestyle. That's not me, and he recognized that I'd never be who he wanted me to be. I'm not looking for pity." I stood and took my bowl to the sink.

Dylan came in while I was rinsing. "You aren't alone. I'm here."

I had *not* been looking for him to say that. "It means I'm going to have to stop managing your band. I can't lug an infant to your shows."

The dish in my hands grew blurry, and I became conscious of the fact that I was crying.

With his hands on my waist, he turned me around to face him. Then he halted the flow of water from the faucet. "Did Thomas really say he saw us?"

I shook my head.

"Why would you—" He stopped talking, but his jaw worked to make several words. None of them came out. "You're not pregnant, are you?"

Again, I shook my head.

"This is that lying compulsion you have, isn't it?"

Shock coursed through me for all of a millisecond, and I realized he knew my secret. "Who told you?"

"Jane let it slip one night. She'd imbibed a little too much, and she asked if you'd lied to me yet. Luma chimed in and told me to ask direct questions that could be answered with one word." No pity waited in the depths of his eyes. He appeared neither pleased nor pissed. It took me a moment to recognize firm patience.

I tried to push him away, but I was trapped between him and the counter. I had no leverage. "So, you were just waiting to trip me up."

"No. When Jane sobered up the next day, she called to tell me you haven't lied in months, that this is the longest you've gone, and that it was because of me you were trying so hard. I have to say—you're quite convincing."

That was not news to me, but I still felt like crap. I'd just said unflattering things about Thomas, and he'd been nothing but kind to me. Even when he dumped me, he'd been compassionate. "Thomas broke up with me because he said I was in love with you, and you wrote all your songs about me. He and I never slept together."

"Never?"

Aware that he was on lie-alert, I answered with one word. "Never. I wanted to wait until the sixth date. We only went out five times."

"Lacey, I need to know—why did you lie to me?"

"I wanted you to leave. You make me feel things, and I don't have control over any of it." I swallowed. "I need to have control over my feelings."

"No," he said. "You don't need to control them. You need to let go and revel, wallow, or whatever—but you need to experience your feelings without fearing them."

I was afraid. I didn't want to be swallowed whole by something inside me. "Lying relieves stress. When I'm anxious, nervous, or afraid, I lie." I shrugged. "Doing it makes me feel better, at least in the moment. Sometimes it makes me feel really good."

"You need to turn to other things that make you feel good. Healthy things that don't hurt you or others." His tender tone and the glimmer in his eyes swept me away.

He kissed me, unleashing all kinds of hungry passion. The anxiety that had controlled me slipped away, replaced with a maelstrom of a different kind. I tugged at his shirt, and he lifted his arms so I could remove it. The smooth glide of his skin felt heavenly under my hands, and the taste of his tongue left me desperate for more.

Breaking off, he moved his lips down my chin to my neck. His hands roamed my hips and back. Then he returned to capture my lips. At the same time, he ran his hands up my sides, raising my arms above my head. When he reversed course, I understood that he wanted them left up there. On his second pass, he lifted my sweatshirt. I wasn't wearing a bra, and his move bared my chest.

As he closed his hand over my breast, I raked my nails across his shoulders. He growled and bit my earlobe. "I've wanted you for so long, Lacey. I just didn't want to rush, make a mistake. I didn't want to get it wrong."

It certainly didn't feel wrong. In my whole life, I'd never felt so right. "I thought you were playing games, and you weren't all that into me." I teased my fingertips above the waistband of his jeans.

"I was into you from the first moment I saw you. It scared me how into you I was." He turned me, placing my back was against his chest. Moving my hair, he kissed a path down my neck.

Chills ran rampant down my spine. He cupped my breasts, sank his teeth into my shoulder, and ground his cock against my ass. I gasped. "I want you inside me."

"You wouldn't happen to have any condoms handy, would you? I came prepared to comfort a friend."

"You're doing a great job so far."

He squeezed my nipple in retribution, but I only moaned and arched against him.

Fortunately, I had a box in my kitchen junk drawer. I'd purchased them in anticipation of my sixth date with Thomas. Being two years out of practice, I hadn't been sure where they should go, and my bathroom cupboards were jammed with shampoo and towels — six of everything. I fumbled for the box, and it took a coordinated effort to open it.

We'd waited too long to draw this out now. I shoved my sweats down and kicked them off one foot. Then I turned and unbuttoned and unzipped Dylan's jeans, shoving them out of the way as he rolled on a condom.

The tattoo of a rosebud greeted me from his upper thigh.

He turned me around again and guided himself in. I braced my hands against the counter and arched my back. The first few strokes were tentative and slow, but with the third thrust, he lifted me off my feet. I moaned and fell forward. He caught me.

"Hang on, Lacey. I'm not going to be very gentle this time."

And he wasn't. He pounded into me, filling my body and my soul. Heat spiraled in my core, and I came much too quickly. Dylan's climax followed mine. He buried himself deeply and stayed there for the longest time. I didn't mind because I never wanted to be apart.

As our bodies cooled, Dylan got rid of the rest of our clothes. My sweats and panties were around one ankle, so I didn't have much left to strip away.

"I'm getting cold."

He lifted me and guided my legs around his waist. "Don't worry; I'll keep you warm. Grab the condoms."

I snagged them as we went by.

"I wrote lyrics to another song about you." He shifted to hold me with one hand so he could open my bedroom door.

"When will I get to hear it?"

He fell onto the bed with me in the middle. "Not sure. I didn't want you to get mad at me again. The other songs were general enough, but this one is pretty specific."

I rolled us so I was on top. Sitting up afforded me a gorgeous view. I touched him slowly, searching out the places that made his eyes turn a darker shade of teal.

"What's it called?"

"Six."

I stuttered in my caresses. "Six. Because I have to wash my hands six times?"

He stroked his palms over my thighs and up to my ribs. "You need six of everything. Or a multiple of six."

"You noticed." I was impressed. Most people didn't pick up on it.

"I like your quirks, but I didn't know if you were touchy about them."

He put a pretty spin on my OCD. I snorted. "Lying isn't a quirk."

"One lie in six months isn't bad, Lacey. Most people tell multiple lies each day. If you look at it that way, you're the most honest person I know." He wet his fingertip and circled my nipple. "Besides, I wasn't talking about that. I was talking about how you need six of everything."

He sat up and closed his hot mouth on my areola. He played with that nub, teasing it to a peak with his teeth and tongue. I fisted my hands in his hair, probably pulling too hard, but I didn't care. By the time he moved on to my other breast, molten need pulsed through my veins. If he was going to keep doing that, I needed something to ride.

The box of condoms had fallen on the mattress next to us. I found one and ripped open the wrapper.

Dylan regarded it with amusement. "I just came. No man recovers that fast."

"It's been ten minutes."

"I need ten more." He flipped me onto my back and kissed a path down my front. "Don't worry; I've read enough lesbian romance novels to know how to keep you occupied for that long."

Finding out he read romance novels wasn't surprising. Him admitting to it did surprise me. Also, the lesbian part. I wanted to know about the lesbian part. "Lesbian romance novels?"

"Yep. Unless it involves my sister, girl-on-girl action is hot. Audra has a huge collection on her tablet, and it's been a lonely year. That, and I can picture you as both of them without some dude's junk getting in the way."

He scooted to lay next to me. The length of him pressed against me, and I took a minute to admire. When my gaze returned to his face, I knew he'd spent the time doing the same thing.

Spreading his hand wide, he slid it from my stomach to my throat. The slow, sensual glide and the sheer possessiveness of the action got me going almost as much as having his mouth on my nipple. Then he reversed direction, not stopping until he made it to the apex of my thighs, and a nudge had me moving my legs apart.

I expected him to go for gold, but he didn't touch my pink places. Instead he massaged my inner thighs, his fingertips moving in kneading spirals that drew ever closer to where I wanted him. I whimpered at his teasing, but he only grinned.

As his thighs were nearby, I slipped my hand between them and gave him back some of what he gave. His cock stirred to life, and I returned his grin.

I'd upped the stakes, and he responded nicely. He slid his fingertips through my wetness, exploring me at a leisurely pace. He circled my clit and stroked the sensitive flesh between there and my entrance. In minutes, he had me close to coming.

"Harder."

He took direction perfectly. I pumped my hips against his hand. Heat built, and I sensed my climax. Careful not to stop him, I grabbed his shoulder. My body bucked, arching off the bed as I shouted.

Before the pulsing stopped, he rolled on the condom I'd been holding and positioned himself between my legs. "I'm going to make you come again."

I wasn't sure if I could. I'd tried this before with Davey and Simon. It hadn't worked. I might not need twenty minutes between rounds, but I did need a few. "Dylan, let me rest for a bit."

He dropped his shoulders and hooked them under my knees. "No rest for the wicked."

The yoga pants I like to wear are mostly for show. I wasn't limber enough to do this. I wanted to protest, but he plunged in, and all I could think about was the way he filled me. He withdrew slowly only to thrust back quickly. Then he would withdraw quickly and thrust back slowly. He didn't set any kind of discernible pattern, and my body couldn't acclimate to his style.

"You're teasing me."

"You teased me for months. This is payback."

"Months? I never teased you."

"Tight shirts." He thrust hard and fast. "Shorts. Short skirts." He withdrew slowly and reversed direction without changing his speed. "Cherry lip gloss—all the fucking time."

I liked my lip gloss, but I hadn't been aware he'd noticed it. That observation/accusation made me inordinately happy. "You like my lip gloss?"

"You taste of it every time I kiss you. I can't eat a goddamn piece of fruit without thinking about you."

"You say the sweetest things."

He leaned forward and put his weight on his hands. My legs slid from his shoulders, down his arms. This left me splayed open, and it released some of the tension on my legs.

"Those leggings you've been wearing recently. They hug your ass. You have an exceptionally nice ass."

I liked the way he gave a compliment. "They're yoga pants. Leggings are tight all the way down."

"Woman, I don't want a fashion lesson."

"Well, then shut up and fuck me."

He did. No more playing around. He made circular motions with his hips and released my legs to suck on my nipples. He kissed the sensitive places on my neck and nibbled my earlobes. I writhed in his arms, coming twice before he finally gave in to his passion.

I wasn't aware of how sweaty we were until he collapsed on top of me. By that point, I was too tired to care.

We must have dozed off because I awoke to the ringing of my cell phone. Dylan had rolled to the side, but his arm and leg were across me, wrapping me and keeping me in his embrace. Gingerly, I tried to move him without waking him, but his limbs were heavy. I ended up shoving them.

He didn't budge. I threw a sleep shirt over my head and looked back to see if he'd stirred. There he was, on my bed, in the place I'd wanted him for so long, still in dreamland. His dark hair was messy, matted in some places and standing on end in others. I looked over his long body, taking in his magnificent shoulders and arms, ass and thighs. I could look at him all day, but my cell chirped to let me know there was a message.

I expected my mother to call, or else I would've let it go. When I got to the living room, it turned out I had three voice messages. Luma, Jane, and my mother had all called. Daisy and Levi had texted me. Gavin had sent me a picture of a kitten.

I listened to my messages, called my mom to assure her I was fine, and returned the texts.

Dylan stumbled out of the bedroom, naked as a jaybird and just as self-conscious. "What are you doing?"

"Well, I posted on KMG's Facebook page that the lead singer has just gotten laid, and you know how your sister trolls that thing.

She texted me a high-five. Of course, some of your fans are pissed. They think you should remain single and available. Others sent you a high-five and requested photos."

He blinked at me. "Was that a joke?"

I wasn't offended. The man was barely awake. "I think it qualifies as a lie."

He nodded. "Okay, good. I'm going to get some water, and then I'm going to jump in the shower. Why don't you join me? I'm not finished with you yet today."

He'd made me come four times. I was impressed that he wanted another round. I finished texting Daisy—she'd wanted to know if Dylan and I were okay—and joined him in the shower.

I found him with his face under the spray. Rivulets ran down his body, highlighting the ripples. Playing guitar and lugging equipment kept him in prime condition. I wrapped my arms around him and snuggled against his back.

"So, am I really the second woman you've slept with?"

"Yep."

My hands tingled. When he moved out of the way, I washed them. This wasn't something I'd done in the shower since I was a teen hiding my habit from my mom and John.

Dylan wrapped his arms around me. "Wanna tell me what you're anxious about?"

"What makes you think I'm anxious?"

"The hand washing is an obvious tell."

"I guess I'm wondering what this afternoon means to you."

He moved out of the spray and searched through my shampoo collection. "Do you have anything that smells manly?"

"Nope. You maybe want to go with the vanilla. It has the lightest scent."

He selected cherry and soaped his hair. When he wrinkled his nose at me, I knew he was considering how to address my concern. "I guess I don't really understand the question."

"You said you came here to support a friend."

"And to bring you chili. I remembered you like it." He rinsed and conditioned. That explained the softness of his hair.

He was purposely leaving me hanging. "Dylan…"

"Feel my face. Tell me if that's too rough for you. I shaved this morning, but sometimes I need to do it again in the evening."

I'd feel his face all right. I'd feel it the way I felt his nose when he wrote that damn song. "If you'd rather not answer, I wish you'd just say so. I don't like games."

He advanced slowly, probably in deference to the slick bathtub. I took small steps back until the tiled wall halted my progress. He took my hands one at a time and lifted them to his cheeks. "Too scratchy? Last chance to weigh in."

They felt fine. I liked them a little scratchy. A five o'clock shadow looked fantastic on Dylan. "Not too scratchy."

Then he pinned my wrists to the wall. "Let's get one thing perfectly clear: I waited because I wanted us both to be sure. I love you, Lacey. Heart and soul. I love everything about you. I love the way you smile, the way you pretend to know what's going on when you haven't been following the conversation, the fact that you need things in groups of six. Don't think I haven't figured out why you want us to hire two backup singers."

That was a connection I hadn't made, but it was true.

"I love your intelligence, your tenacity, and your wit. I love your zest for life and the way you have unfailingly believed in me from the start." He released my hands and turned to rinse his hair. "Did that adequately answer your question?"

More than. I nodded, but he couldn't see me. "Dylan?"

He finished and turned back to me. "Yeah?"

"I love you too."

His cocky grin was worth it. "I was thinking."

I caressed his head. "Does it hurt?"

"Funny. As I said, I love your sense of humor." His face hovered inches above mine. "I think you shouldn't deliver your lies so convincingly. Give a mischievous smile at the end to let people know you're joking. Or use some of your dry wit. Make it ironic or sarcastic. It'll provide the stress relief you need without the stigma of a lie."

The idea held appeal. "I'll think about it."

He dropped to his knees. I hoped he wasn't going to propose in my shower.

"Hold on to the towel bar."

I barely had time to grab it before he threw my knee over his shoulder and buried his face between my legs. Holy hell, that man had a talented tongue and strong lips. He supported my ass with one hand and added the fingers of his other to the mix. They curled inside me, finding my sweet spot with every stroke.

"The towel bar isn't going to hold me," I warned him.

His chuckle turned to a moan when I grabbed his hair for leverage and rode his face into the sunset.

Chapter Eighteen

Dinner was delicious, not that I tasted it much. We made grilled cheese sandwiches with tomato and bacon, and it turned out I was ravenous. I inhaled my food, finishing well before Dylan, and after that, our conversation meandered. He talked about recording the band's first EP. I'd booked studio time for them next month. I talked about John — a lot. I opened up and told Dylan all the things I'd withheld before.

"I was terrified of him at first. It took three weeks before I stopped hiding under a table in the corner with a plastic sword in my hands."

I couldn't tell whether Dylan wanted to laugh or hug me. He took a sip of milk. "They didn't place you with a female counselor so you'd feel more comfortable?"

I studied Dylan closely. What did the gender of my therapist have to do with anything? "What did I say — exactly — in the bathroom yesterday?"

He shrugged. "You said enough for me to figure things out."

I couldn't have said nearly enough. I regarded him somberly and confessed the details of my sordid past. He listened, his fists clenching and angry color rising to his cheeks at several points, but he didn't comment or interrupt.

The apartment was silent for a full minute after I stopped talking. I knew what he was doing. Counselors are trained to let the quiet make people talk. However, I'd said it all.

"Wow," he finally said. "I knew you were a strong woman. Looks like you've been that way your entire life."

"I don't always feel strong." My mother is a fierce woman. I don't have a tenth of her strength. She lost her husband, and it hadn't destroyed her. That amazed me. I felt adrift without John, though now I had Dylan to anchor me. "Right now I feel very, very weak."

He pulled me onto his lap and held me in the safe cocoon of his arms. "It still hits me like that sometimes. Losing a parent is hard. You don't have to pretend with me. Ever."

After breakfast, Dylan sang the song he'd been working on.

She's pretty and she's smart
Completely unaware.
Six smiles
Six laughs
Six kisses on the lips
She hears whispers in the dark
Telling her she's loved

Six notes
Six chords
Six lines I write
Six roses
Six bridesmaids
Six layers on the cake
Six lines our vows
Six seconds our kiss
Six days the trip

She's pretty and she's smart
Completely unaware.
Six smiles
Six laughs
Six kisses on the lips
She hears whispers in the dark
Telling her she's loved

Six bedrooms in the house
Six kids come along
Six times I take her
In my arms
Six times I whisper…

I had no words, only tears. He made love to me one more time. (Six total orgasms, and yes, he was counting—that sweet, sweet man.)

Later, I shoved him out the door. "You need to go home and get some fresh clothes before you can see patients today."

He hesitated, a protest in the firm set of his jaw.

"I'm fine. I have a meeting. I need to see my mother, and then we have a band meeting at seven at your house. I'll be over at seven."

And I was fine for the moment. I held it together until I arrived at my mother's house. John had almost always answered the door when I came over. Seeing my mom assume that duty socked me in the gut.

Mom must have known because she pushed open the screen and pulled me into her safe, familiar embrace. "Baby, I know. Come in. I have some tea made, and there's a shitload of food in the kitchen. People apparently think I buried my ability to cook."

My mother's sense of humor was intact. I wanted to ask how she was doing—wasn't that the polite thing?—but I knew the answer. Humor was her shield. I don't know how many times she found gun jokes to tell me when I was growing up. John did his best to rein her in, but my mother was a force in and of herself.

She set a cup of lemon tea in front of me and gave me an envelope. "John left you this. After his heart attack, he put his affairs in order, and he wrote some notes. I gave one to each of his sisters, one to his nephew, a couple to close friends. I didn't read them, though."

I opened the envelope to find a handwritten note.

Dear Lacey,

Words cannot describe the blessings you've brought to my life, but I'm going to try anyway. I knew from an early age that I could never have children. I'm not a religious man, but I can't deny that something divine sent us to each other. You say all the time how I helped you, but you healed me too. You wouldn't remember this, but when I met you, I was this hotshot therapist who had absolutely nothing but his work. I had no friends, no real connection with my family. I had loads of acquaintances, and nobody to love. I thought I was "all that" because I listened to people whine about their petty problems all day and offered solutions.

Working with you challenged my core beliefs, my cynicism about people. You have grit, a stubborn tenacity I hadn't seen before. You showed me I had more to give to people than a bill at the end of fifty minutes. You humbled me. You showed me what it was like to work for love — real love. Because of you, I met your mother, and of course you know, she is the great love of my life.

If you're reading this, I've passed on. I want you to know that I'm proud of you — of everything you do and everything you are. I wish I could be beside you to see the great things you're going to do with your life. Know that I will never leave your side. I might not be there in body, but I'll always be there in spirit. I love you, Lacey. You might not have called me "Dad," but you are my little girl. You always will be.

By the time I finished reading, the words were blurry with tears. I sobbed like a baby, and my mom held me with my face pressed to her abdomen, just like she used to. She didn't say anything as the pain knifed through me. She just rubbed my back and shoulder until I was all cried out.

When I looked up, I saw her tears. I sat up, putting my arms around her.

We didn't eat lunch. Neither of us was hungry. Instead we sipped tea and reminisced about the man we adored. Sadie kept us company by napping under the table.

On the way out, I casually mentioned that Dylan and I were together.

She stared at me, skepticism written all over her face. "What about Thomas?"

"We broke up."

"Really? After he flew all the way here to be by your side?"

"I swear I'm telling the truth. Thomas and I talked yesterday morning. He told me he couldn't be with a woman who was in love with another man."

She rolled her eyes. "John predicted this. He said one day you'd realize what your heart truly wanted, and you wouldn't waste time once you did."

I waited silently, hoping she'd give me her blessing.

She didn't disappoint. "Dylan is a good man. And if the band thing doesn't work out, he has a good degree to fall back on."

Now came a task I didn't relish. During my short leave from work, I had neglected to tell the band some important information.

Dylan met me as I walked up the driveway. I was used to letting myself into the house and going straight down to the basement. I didn't have a key, but they kept the side door unlocked. He greeted me with a light kiss on the lips and walked with me the rest of the way.

"I didn't say anything about us to the band. I thought maybe you'd want to tell them together."

Truthfully, I hadn't thought about breaking the news to the band. I dodged the question. "I told my mother."

He shoved a hand in his jeans pocket. "What did she say?"

"She said you're a good man." The first day of November was cold, and I was tired. I tried to move past him into the house, but he caught my arm.

"You've been crying."

Great. Did that mean my face looked puffy and my eyes were bloodshot? "My mom gave me a letter John wrote."

"Are you okay?"

I shrugged. "Like you said—one minute I'm fine, and the next I feel like somebody sucker-punched me."

"Did you want to—"

"Dylan, can we just do this meeting first? I have real business to discuss. I assure you nobody is going to be surprised. When I told Daisy about Thomas, she was a little mad at me because she thought you and I were already dating."

"Oh." He held the door for me. I went inside and let the air warm the chill in my bones. "I was going to ask if you wanted to postpone the meeting. If you're not feeling up to it, nobody's going to blame you."

Now I felt like an ass. "I'm sorry. I shouldn't have jumped on you like that."

He grinned. "I'll let you make it up to me later, maybe by jumping on me naked."

"It's about time." Gavin's comment made me blush.

The back door opened to a landing that led to the basement stairs. In the other direction, one step led up to the kitchen. It was a blind corner. While I could see the refrigerator, I couldn't see the rest of the room. Apparently, it contained Gavin.

"Seriously? Now we're gonna get a series of sappy love songs."

That came from Levi. I peered up at Dylan. "Problem solved."

Daisy came up the stairs and whacked Dylan's ass on her way to the kitchen. "Proud of you, little brother. You're not going to die a lonely, born-again virgin."

I'm sure my face was crimson. I buried it in Dylan's chest.

Daisy pried me away from him. She kissed me on the cheek. "Welcome to the family, sister."

I gave her a sassy smile. "Sister? Does this mean I get to borrow your clothes?"

We climbed the single step into the kitchen to find Levi and Gavin chuckling quietly.

"What's so funny?" I asked.

Levi's shoulders shook harder.

Dylan punched Levi's arm. "You better not have made bets."

Gavin lost his battle first. Laughter burst from him.

I looked to Daisy, but she just shook her head. I didn't take that to mean she had no idea what was going on, only that she wanted no part of it.

Levi cleared his throat. "Back before we asked you to be our manager, we all bet on how long it would take you two to hook up. Monty cleaned our clocks. Looks like we all owe him forty bucks."

"Monty was in on it? That little shit." There was no heat in Dylan's exclamation, yet Daisy glared at him anyway.

"He happens to be very good at reading people," she said. "He argued that you would drag your feet until something forced you to make a move."

"I thought you'd cave the moment you found out she was seeing somebody else," Gavin said.

I saw where this was heading, and I didn't want to go there. This group could derail a meeting faster than a cat can lick its ass. This was as good a time as any to throw some more onto their collective plate. "So, I forgot to call and schedule dates for the three record producers to stop by."

Beneath the sympathetic expressions, I saw an undercoating of trepidation.

"It seems RCA and Dreamworks didn't wait for me. They sent reps to see your last concert." It had been the day before John's funeral. "And they both want to meet with you. I think you should meet with them both, hear them out, and then decide if you want to go with a label or go indie."

I wondered if I'd lost the counsel of Patrick Westman when I'd lost Thomas. I certainly knew there was no way Thomas would read over the contract for me. He was a great guy, but he had his limits.

Dylan went to throw his arms around me, but Daisy got there first. "Oh, hell yes, you can borrow my clothes."

I was ripped from her arms by Gavin. "I knew we were right to beg you to come back."

Levi took his turn. "You're our good luck charm, Lacey."

Dylan, wise man, waited until they finished their round of celebratory hugging to wrap his arms around me. He smacked a kiss on my lips. "I'm going to call my next song 'Cherry Kisses' after the way you taste."

"See?" Levi said. "What did I tell you? Love songs. Sappy, happy love songs."

Dylan grinned. "Lots of them." Then he kissed me again, deeper and longer.

Later that evening, after Dylan made love to me, he held me in his arms. "I love you, Lacey — endlessly."

I kissed his shoulder. "I'm not sure that's a romantic sentiment. Isn't that song about the death of hope?"

He strummed his fingertips over my back, tickling a little and leaving gooseflesh in his wake. "I think it's about beating the odds because you know the one you love will always be there waiting for you — no matter what crap misery throws at you. That's what gave me the fortitude to wait until you found your way back to me."

I lifted my head to look at his face. He is a consummate romantic. I need him by my side to point me to all the wonders life has to offer.

"I like your interpretation much better than mine. I love you, Dylan — endlessly."

Acknowledgments

I could not have done this without the support and encouragement of some key players. Thanks to Suzy for telling me it was okay to try a new genre. Thanks to my kids for being considerate when I need to work. I don't have an office or any place designated for writing, so they've been great at giving me space and sometimes making me stop to play with them.

In the writing world, I met Katie Mac and the Indie Express. When I needed beta readers, she put together a rocking group of people who gave me invaluable feedback and advice. They fell in love with Dylan and Lacey, and words cannot express how much that meant to me! Thanks to Amy Malek Concepcion, Becky Schmidt, Lara Feldstein, Julie B. Deaton, Lea Burn, and Jennifer Diaz for your painstaking efforts and detailed notes! Lacey was a difficult character to get right, and you definitely helped me realize my vision for her.

About the Author

I'm Michele Zurlo, author of more than twenty romance novels. I write contemporary and paranormal, BDSM and mainstream—whatever it takes to give my characters the happy endings they deserve.

I'm not half as interesting as my characters. My childhood dreams tended to stretch no further than the next book in my to-be-read pile, and I aspired to be a librarian so I could read all day. I ended up teaching middle school, so that fulfilled part of my dream. Some words of wisdom from an inspiring lady had me tapping out stories on my first laptop, so these days, in the evenings, romantic tales flow from my fingertips.

I'm pretty impulsive when it comes to big decisions, especially when it's something I've never done before. Writing is just one in a long line of impulsive decisions that turned out to showcase my great instincts.☺ Find out more at www.michelezurloauthor.com or @MZurloAuthor.

Sneak Peek of
Kiss Me By Moonlight

On the way home, Dylan fumed silently. I drove, as he tends to speed and cut people off when he's in a sour mood. We were almost to my apartment when he said, "Aren't you going to apologize?"

I glanced at him, surprised he'd ask me to lie. "I'm sorry?"

"That's not going to cut it."

"I'm not sorry I said it. I'm sorry I hurt your feelings, but you know how I feel about that song." I turned into the parking lot and found the space designated for my apartment.

"You called me a manwhore, Lacey." His entire life, Dylan had slept with two women, one of whom was his late wife. "That's not the image we're trying to project. We want fans to focus on our music, not our imagined bedroom antics."

I got out of the car. This seems to be another "discussion" Dylan wants to have. You know what I'm spoiling for? An all-out fight. There's a lot of pent-up frustration and anger mixed with residual hurt and grief inside me, and that much emotion is going to demand an outlet if I don't provide one.

On the plus side, the fact that I want to argue, scream, and yell bodes well for the conditions of my hands. Perhaps that's why Dylan listed those options for me earlier. He knew what I wanted before I did. I kind of resent him for that. People you're mad at aren't supposed to be right or accommodating. Dylan manages to be both. Manwhore.

He followed me into the apartment, hopefully noting the stiffness of my shoulders. I projected outrage as hard as I could. Lies to cover lies. I know what I did was wrong, and that it wasn't a little problem. I'd said it in front of the media. Not for the first time, I considered that I was a bad choice to manage his band. My mouth was bound to garner negative press.

I went into my bedroom and into the closet. It's a large, walk-in number half full of his clothes. I went to my dress section and began evaluating which one I would wear to see John's grave. Though it had been chilly when we left this morning at an ungodly hour, the sun had come out for the return trip and warmed things up considerably. The ice in the parking lot was melting, and the early spring day promised to get even warmer. I selected a long-sleeved black velvet shirt and its matching full-length skirt.

Dylan stood in the door of the closet, blocking my path. He eyed the dress in my hand incredulously. "What the hell are you doing?"

I responded with a passively neutral expression. "Changing."

This is my way of goading him. He has a temper, but it takes a lot to get him to explode. I have a hard time expressing anger, and I hate how Dylan gets eerily calm when he deals with me. This is my way of compelling him to force me to let it out. Fucked up, right?

He took the clothes from me and threw them on the floor, which was littered with shoes. Then he gripped my chin in his cupped hand, making me face him. "No. We're going to discuss whatever is eating you up."

I tried to shake my head, but he didn't let me move. "I'm fine."

"Liar. You're so not fine, it's not even funny. I haven't seen you this way in months."

If I take a step back, he'll let go of me and back off. I stared at him, wondering who was going to break first.

He studied me, searching my eyes for answers I didn't have. "You weren't calling me a name; you were lying."

"It's a fine line, isn't it?" I spoke softly, my eyes locked to his. "And at the end of the day, it doesn't actually matter."

"No," he agreed, releasing my chin. "It doesn't. The damage is done. You're going to have to deal with the fallout to make this right."

I am not prepared to handle public relations, but I nodded anyway. Tonight I'm supposed to hang with Jane and Luma. I'll spill my tale of woe and ask for advice. Luma has a degree in public relations. She'll have some ideas.

He tried to take me in his arms, but I stiffened and pulled away. The whirligig of crappy emotions hadn't left the building. Dylan wasn't nearly as pissed as he should be.

He sighed. "You're a difficult woman to live with."

I put my hands on my hips and squared up to him. "I never asked you to live here."

←→New Adult←→

Three Daves by Nicki Elson
Streamline by Jennifer Lane
Shades of Atlantis by Carol Oates
The Heart series: *Beside Your Heart* & *Disclosure of the Heart*
by Mary Whitney
Romancing the Bookworm by Kate Evangelista
Fighting Fate by Linda Kage
Flirting with Chaos by Kenya Wright
The Vice, Virtue & Video series: *Revealed* (book 1) by Bianca Giovanni

←→Erotic Romance←→

The Keyhole series: *Becoming sage* (book one) by Kasi Alexander
The Keyhole series: *Saving sunni* (book two) by Kasi & Reggie Alexander
The Winemaker's Dinner: *Appetizers* & *Entrée* by Dr. Ivan Rusilko & Everly Drummond
The Winemaker's Dinner: *Dessert* by Dr. Ivan Rusilko
Client N° 5 by Joy Fulcher

←→Paranormal Romance←→

The Light series: *Seers of Light, Whisper of Light* & *Circle of Light*
by Jennifer DeLucy
The Hanaford Park series: *Eve of Samhain* & *Pleasures Untold* by Lisa Sanchez
Immortal Awakening by KC Randall
The Seraphim series: *Crushed Seraphim* & *Bittersweet Seraphim*
by Debra Anastasia
The Guardian's Wild Child by Feather Stone
Grave Refrain by Sarah M. Glover
Divinity by Patricia Leever
Blood Vine series: *Blood Vine* & *Blood Entangled* & *Blood Reunited* by Amber
Belldene
Divine Temptation by Nicki Elson
Love in the Time of the Dead by Tera Shanley

←→Historical Romance←→

Cat O' Nine Tails by Patricia Leever
Burning Embers by Hannah Fielding
Good Ground by Tracy Winegar

Romantic Suspense

Whirlwind by Robin DeJarnett
The CONduct series: *With Good Behavior* & *Bad Behavior* &
On Best Behavior by Jennifer Lane
Indivisible by Jessica McQuinn
Between the Lies by Alison Oburia

Anthologies

A Valentine Anthology including short stories by
Alice Clayton ("With a Double Oven"),
Jennifer DeLucy ("Magnus of Pfelt, Conquering Viking Lord"),
Nicki Elson ("I Don't Do Valentine's Day"),
Jessica McQuinn ("Better Than One Dead Rose and a Monkey Card"),
Victoria Michaels ("Home to Jackson"), and
Alison Oburia ("The Bridge")

Singles and Novellas

It's Only Kinky the First Time (Keyhole series) by Kasi Alexander
Learning the Ropes (Keyhole series) by Kasi & Reggie Alexander
The Winemaker's Dinner: RSVP by Dr. Ivan Rusilko
The Winemaker's Dinner: No Reservations by Everly Drummond
Big Guns by Jessica McQuinn
Concessions by Robin DeJarnett
Starstruck by Lisa Sanchez
New Flame by BJ Thornton
Shackled by Debra Anastasia
Swim Recruit by Jennifer Lane
Sway by Nicki Elson
Full Speed Ahead by Susan Kaye Quinn
The Second Sunrise by Hannah Downing
The Summer Prince by Carol Oates
Whatever it Takes by Sarah M. Glover
Clarity (A *Divinity* prequel single) by Patricia Leever
A Christmas Wish (A *Cocktails & Dreams* single) by Autumn Markus
Late Night with Andres by Debra Anastasia